"Fleu... you leave here."

There was a threatening conclusiveness in Elliot's words, and Fleur stared at him, fear pressing like a rock against her windpipe.

"That's abduction," she whispered, a pulse beating furiously at her temple. "You could get a prison sentence for that."

"Maybe," he grated, his breathing shallow, "but don't imagine that Steadman's isn't worth it. It is." He bent toward her, one hand on the arm of the settee, the other just above her shoulder, imprisoning her there. In a hazy panic, she noticed the full sensuality of his cruel mouth, the dangerous gleam in his eyes, and she shrank back, sensing his determination.

"You've no power to keep me here against my will," she said desperately, but fear raced through her like wildfire as she realized that he could.

Elizabeth Power was once a legal secretary, but when the compulsion to write became too strong, she abandoned affidavits, wills and conveyances in favor of a literary career. Her husband, she says, is her best critic. And he's a good cook, too—often readily taking over the preparation of meals when her writing is in full flow. They live in a three-hundred-year-old English country estate cottage, surrounded by woodlands and wildlife. Who wouldn't be inspired to write?

Rude Awakening
Elizabeth Power

Harlequin Books

TORONTO • NEW YORK • LONDON
AMSTERDAM • PARIS • SYDNEY • HAMBURG
STOCKHOLM • ATHENS • TOKYO • MILAN

Original hardcover edition published in 1986
by Mills & Boon Limited

ISBN 0-373-02825-3

Harlequin Romance first edition March 1987

CHAPTER ONE

EVERYONE had gone home at last. From the sixth floor of Steadman International, Fleur Galaway watched the blur of stationary red lights in the darkness below her window, grimacing at the rain streaming down the outside of the pane. London's evening rush hour was already heralding its peak with the usual blare of car horns and tonight, a torrential downpour! she thought wryly, her attention suddenly caught by the lazy whine of a lift descending at the far end of the corridor.

She turned her blonde head towards the door and the warm cocoon of dark offices beyond it and listened. Nothing. Good. Now she could get the information David had asked for.

With a purposeful stride she moved across to the computer, her high-heeled shoes making no sound on the carpeted floor, long hair draped like a platinum curtain over her shoulder as she studied the slip of paper she took out of her desk.

Phoenix. At the computer her fingers sought the relevant keys for the code name necessary to retrieve the privileged information and her thoughts went back to what David had said that afternoon.

'Use absolute discretion. Wait until the others have gone,' she remembered him advising her. Well he'd meant simply Stacey and June, she reflected, glancing across at the covered typewriters and closed accounts files, but she couldn't get any more discreet than this. The whole sixth floor was as deserted as a ghost ship!

Or was it? She paused, ears straining, every nerve alert, her fingers suddenly freezing over the keys.

Someone was standing in the doorway—watching her!
And quickly she looked up, her startled eyes meeting the
questioning grey of the man's in the shadowy aperture.

'Working late, Fleur?'

Tall, dark, and with that unmistakable air of command, Elliot Steadman strode in wearing a curious half
smile, the kind that had been raising female tempera-
tures over the past two months from junior level to
personnel, but Fleur's heart plummeted. David had
particularly requested that she didn't let Elliot know
what she was doing for him, but the chairman was going
to find out for himself if he came any closer. It was crazy,
but she felt like a criminal!

'I-I thought you were away?' she stammered. Office
rumour had it that he had taken a few days off to move
house, so what was he doing here? she thought,
swallowing hard. Why didn't he stay where he was?

But he walked straight over to the computer, thick
brows knit as he scanned the visual display unit, and
something frightening leapt in his eyes as he digested the
information on the sheet of paper beside it.

'Obviously,' he said tersely, answering her. He picked
up the note David had dictated to her earlier and despite
her sinking heart she noticed how long and well-tapered
his hands were, and tanned, too, against the crisp
whiteness of his shirt cuff. 'What the hell do you think
you're doing with this?' The accusation in his voice cut
sharply into her thoughts. His eyes were hard beneath his
thick, dark eyebrows, and a muscle tightened in the
strong jaw. 'This is confidential information. How the
hell did you get hold of it?'

Fleur gulped, Elliot's mood rendering her speechless.
David had warned her that the chairman would be angry
if he found out what she was doing for him, because he'd
been lax—let things slide again—she thought, exaspera-
tedly, failing to brief himself with this information when

he was supposed to. Was that why Elliot was so annoyed? Because his top sales executive hadn't done his home-work—*again*?

'I'm waiting, Fleur.' The deep voice assured her he would go on waiting—and all night—if he had to. Well, Elliot Steadman was just going to have to work it out for himself. Couldn't he simply accept that it was David who had given her the information—he must have guessed by now—without forcing her to admit the younger man's increasing inefficiency? That would be like telling tales out of school.

'You'd better start explaining yourself.'

Cagily Fleur glanced up at six feet plus of dominant masculinity. His arms were folded across his broad chest and the dark, well-cut suit he was wearing emphasised the narrowness of his waist, the leanness of his hips and the muscular strength of his thighs. 'However you got hold of that information you know you've no right being in possession of it. Now or at any time!' There was a cold, seething anger behind his words and Fleur swallowed again as their true meaning registered itself.

At any time? Suddenly she felt sick. Had David requested data from her knowing full well that she shouldn't have access to it, rather than come in here and get the information he required personally? Had his increasing laxity in the office led him into doing something that could get them both into trouble?

'I'm well aware that it's confidential,' she started, 'but . . .' What could she say? She dropped her hands into her lap, toying with the soft, white wool of her dress. What explanation could she possibly offer him without making things bad for David?

'Only four members of the company knew about that password.' Angrily, Elliot jerked his head towards the visual display. 'Apart from my father and myself. Three of those are away at the moment, which leaves Andrew

Moreton ... and I think I know him well enough to assume that he wouldn't have leaked this information by accident or any other way ...' He dropped down to her level, hands flat on the desk, his face so close to hers that she could smell the lemony spice of his aftershave lotion. 'And my father ... as you very well know, *Miss* Galaway, is dead.' He spoke slowly and deliberately, every deep syllable perfectly pronounced, and Fleur touched her top lip with her tongue, unsettled by the total maleness of him—the condemnation she read in his murky grey eyes.

'So ...' He straightened, towering and formidable beside her. 'Your ingenuity with computers and your ... ambitions ... obviously include dipping into company secrets!'

Blonde hair swished wildly as she swung to face him. 'That's not true!'

'Isn't it?' Elliot thrust the piece of paper he was still holding towards her. 'Then how do you explain this?'

Her throat constricting, Fleur slumped back on her chair. David. He'd given her that password. Told her, when he'd asked for her discretion, that only top level management and executives knew anything about it. Well, he *was* a top level executive, she thought, baffled. But Elliot hadn't mentioned his name just now. So what was going on? And what was so important about Phoenix anyway?

'I think you'd better come with me.'

The deep, male voice intruded unnervingly upon her thoughts and she stared up at him incredulously, her full lips parted in disbelief.

'What?' she whispered.

'I said you'd better come with me,' he repeated, inexorably. And suddenly the seriousness of her predicament struck her.

Elliot was as good as accusing her of being an

industrial spy! And there was no way that she could prove that she wasn't unless she told him that David was responsible for giving her that information. And she couldn't do that. Not yet. Not until she had spoken to him. He was her cousin—no, more than that, she thought, remembering the bond that had once existed between them when they had been as close as brother and sister. He could never be mixed up in anything underhand . . . could he? Colour drained out of her fine-boned cheeks, and she felt her palms growing hot and sweaty. Surely he wouldn't involve her in anything wrong. Not David. Please not David! There had to be some mistake.

'Oh I hope there's been some mistake...' She dropped her face into her hand, her elbow supported by the desk. Her head was beginning to swim in a sickening maelstrom of confusion. 'I-I can't think . . .'

Strong, hard fingers were taking control, gripping her arm, dragging her up from her chair.

'Get your coat,' Elliot ordered roughly, switching off the computer and thrusting her in front of him away from the machine. 'You'll be dealt with no more leniently than you deserve.'

Amber-flecked brown eyes appealed to him with a mixture of torture, anger and bewilderment.

'Where are you taking me?' He couldn't just bundle her off like this. Or perhaps he thought he could.

With a cool courtesy he helped her on with her coat and she shuddered from his threatening nearness as his hands came to rest firmly on her shoulders.

'I think I'm the one entitled to the answers, don't you?'

Fleur spun round, weakening from the dominance of his height. Even at five feet seven, with three inch heels, she barely reached that strong, thrusting jaw.

'Look . . . I know how it looks,' she admitted, her voice shaking. 'But it isn't at all like it seems.' If only she could have a few minutes alone to use the phone. Talk to her cousin. There had to be a simple explanation to all this. 'I wasn't trying to steal any of the firm's secrets for money or ambition . . . or whatever you're thinking. I obtained that password in complete innocence . . .'

'And you expect me to believe that?' A hard mouth twisted in cruel disdain. Shivering, Fleur turned up the collar of her trench coat, clasping it tightly in a self-protective gesture as she was ushered out of the office and along the quiet corridor. Of course he didn't believe it! She looked as guilty as sin in his eyes, so much so that she was beginning to feel as if she really had committed a crime!

'It's the truth,' she stressed, with all the conviction of her innocence as they stepped into the waiting lift.

Elliot didn't answer. His expression was implacable as he pressed the button for the ground floor, and from beneath her eyelashes Fleur studied him discreetly.

Thirty-five, that's all he was. Only twelve years older than she was, yet seeming to possess a lifetime's seniority. Dark-haired, strong-featured and striking, that cool exterior of his masked a shrewd brain she'd have given anything rather than to have tangled with. It had given him control of a vast electronics empire, she reflected, shuddering from the sure knowledge that even if Frank Steadman hadn't died two months ago and left everything to his son, Elliot Steadman would have made it to the top solely on the merits of his own forcefulness and determination. There was a hard maturity about him, she thought, her gaze moving unwittingly over his profile, a ruthlessness in the thrust of that jaw, in the rugged cheek embellished by that flat, dark mole, in the cruel, sensual line of his mouth . . .

She started, aware that he was looking at her with cold contempt, but something else too, which made her startlingly conscious of a dark and brooding sensuality.

She felt a ridiculous burning in her cheeks—a strange uneasiness at being in such a confined space with him— and agitatedly she tore her gaze away to stare at the lighting panel as the button for the ground floor lit up.

'Good night, sir.'

An obsequious night-security man touched his cap as they passed through the foyer of the prestigious glass building, his subsequent 'Night, miss,' only forthcoming, Fleur guessed, because she was with the most illustrious member of the firm. Normally the man couldn't be bothered to speak to her.

'Where are you taking me?' It was a tremulous demand as they stepped through the revolving doors where, beyond the shelter of the portico, the rain was still coming down in torrents. 'I have a right to know.'

'Have you?' There was a sceptical lift to the thick eyebrow, a harsh denial in his voice, before he said grimly, 'Somewhere where you can provide me with some answers. Perhaps a strong drink will loosen your tongue.'

Fleur's first thought was to run. She could get away from him now! Get to a telephone! But he had caught her arm and she was forced to go with him, running like mad through the torrential autumn rain.

Under the lights of the multi-storey car park she could see the heavy raindrops gleaming darkly on Elliot's jacket, one or two rivulets running down his cheek from his thick, black hair. Her own was soaked already, and a droplet cascaded off and ran down her neck inside her coat, making her shiver. She felt wretched and cold.

'Get in.'

Seeing the determination in his face, Fleur complied without argument, and settled herself into the passenger side of the black Jaguar XJS. So he was going to make her talk by pouring alcohol down her was he? she thought, as he reversed out of the space marked

'Chairman'. Well if she was guilty of anything perhaps that would work. But she wasn't. And she knew a sudden, overwhelming feeling of panic. Whatever could she say to him that wouldn't blatantly implicate David? She knew he couldn't be guilty of doing anything against the firm. One of the others must have authorised him to get that information legitimately. If only she could get to a phone!

'What were you possibly hoping to gain tonight, Fleur?' They were on the road, the luxurious, powerful car weaving its way through the late traffic, its brilliant lights reflecting on the wet tarmac, and in its dark interior Elliot's voice had taken on a more persuasive note—more intimate—evident from the way he had breathed her name. Perhaps he hoped a more caressing approach might bring him results, she thought, more affected than she cared to admit by the subtle sensuality behind it. 'Were you planning to sell the information to Stover's . . . give them the benefit of Steadman's hard work and knowhow for a nice, fat, personal profit?'

She glanced at him, puzzled. What did he mean? Stover Electronics *was* Steadman's biggest competitor, but what connection did it have with all this? 'I don't know what you're talking about,' she answered, guilelessly.

'Don't you?' Elliot's words came back like gunshot, all persuasion gone. He was looking at her with eyes so steely cold they frightened her. 'A new component. A contract worth millions which Stover's would dearly love to get their hands on. I think you know what I'm talking about, Fleur.' His eyes were back on the road, needing all the concentration he could give on the wet surface. 'Just how much were they offering you for such privileged information?'

Fleur stared across the dark space between them. So that was what it was all about. A new, secret piece of technology. A big contract. Big money. And he thought she was responsible for trying to sell the deal to the firm's biggest rival! It would have been laughable had his accusation not been such a deadly serious fact.

'They haven't offered me anything,' she rejoined quickly, 'because I'm not guilty of a thing.'

'No?' His tone strongly implied that he still didn't believe her. The traffic was flowing more freely now and Elliot pressed his foot harder to the floor. 'May I point out,' he said, cuttingly, 'that the law sees only a thin line between what is considered ethically wrong and that which is criminal in industrial duplicity. The authorities might well take the dimmer view in the light of the vast sums of money your . . . ambitions . . . are likely to cost me. Perhaps you'd be more willing to co-operate with them.'

Fleur glanced up at him quickly, his words suddenly sinking in. She knew, she hadn't done anything wrong. But what about David? She turned her anxious gaze towards the windscreen, to the wiperblades coping at dual speed with the heavy rain. Was he guilty of something that could eventually lead him to prison? Her throat felt terribly dry, and she licked her lips, longing for a drink of water. She had to be crazy thinking like this. Of course he hadn't done anything wrong. There had to be a perfectly rational explanation for this gross misunderstanding, as she'd find out if only she could find some way to contact him.

'Obviously you hadn't considered the consequences of being caught.' Elliot's voice filtered through her thoughts and she blinked hard, trying to shake herself out of her daze. In a minute she'd wake up and find that this was all some crazy dream.

'Snap out of it!' His voice came again, stern and authoritative, jerking her back to sensibility. 'I've no inclination to treat you for shock.'

'I'm all right,' she gulped, that statement being anything but true. Nervously, she began toying with her wristwatch. 'Are you taking me to the police?'

'Not yet.' Someone with a coat over his head darted out in front of them, causing Elliot to brake hard, and he cursed under his breath. 'You owe your explanations and apologies to me first and by Heaven I intend to have them.'

His determination was unnerving and Fleur shivered. She had guessed when she had first laid eyes on him only two months before that he could be a hard man to cross; that behind that suavè veneer was a man who could build empires or break people with a whiplash of merciless power. Well, now the total potency of his anger was directed against her, and if he wanted explanations she knew without a measure of doubt that he would get them. Just how he might go about it was beginning to scare her silly and suddenly, angry with David for putting her into this predicament, breathlessly she burst out, 'I want to make a phone call.'

'I'll bet you do.' There was cruel mockery in Elliot's tone, but he didn't stop the car. Instead he dropped his foot hard on the accelerator to take the open stretch of dual-carriageway, saying acridly, 'Hoping to find solace in your charming confederate's arms?'

What on earth did he mean by that? Fleur bit down hard on her lower lip until it hurt. How had she ever got into this mess?

'I believe you took a rather exotic holiday back in the summer?' Elliot surprised her by remarking suddenly. 'Something rather extravagant on a computer operator's pay, wouldn't you agree?' He sent her a scathing look. 'Two weeks in Miami, wasn't it?'

Hot colour stole across Fleur's cheeks. That holiday had been the outcome of years of saving—an intended 'thank you' gift to her aunt for bringing her up single-handed after Fleur's own parents had been killed. And that 'thank you' had been expressed not a day too soon because Agnes Markham had died shortly afterwards. Remembering brought scalding tears to Fleur's eyes. But why should she even try explaining that to Elliot when he had already made up his mind that she was a crook?

'So?' she couldn't help retorting heatedly.

'Yes . . . so. And at my bloody expense!'

'That's not true!' she threw back, swallowing emotion. 'I've never taken anything from you . . . or your precious company!'

'It is a year you've been with us, isn't it?' he asked, surprisingly changing the subject again. She didn't answer. He already knew. And with hurt rebellion in her eyes she watched him swing the powerful car off the dual-carriageway towards the more affluent suburbs. 'Whoever interviewed you was obviously too blinded by that sensuous body of yours to see the character behind the fancy casing. Had I been around to interview you you wouldn't have even made the short list.'

Fresh anger coursed along her veins, mingling with confusion and the pain of injustice. 'Had you been around to interview me I wouldn't even have considered the post!' she retaliated, feeling the pinch of his words, but more the unsettling sensation that those condemning grey eyes had just undressed her with one cursory glance. Absurdly she felt her colour rise and turned to stare out at the rain streaming down the window, trying to regain her equilibrium.

She was being utterly stupid, she thought. Flinging insults at the Chairman of the Board was no way to keep her job. But did she want her job after tonight? More to the point, would the Board even consider her worthy of her position of trust if she were found to have played a part, however innocently, in someone else's attempt to cheat the firm?

'I'd appreciate it if you didn't mention this to Elliot if he drops by.' Through the silent darkness her cousin's words came startlingly to mind. Had there been some ulterior motive behind that request other than to avoid his boss's discovery of further inefficiency? she wondered, her throat constricting. But no, there couldn't be, she told herself with strong conviction. David wasn't capable of anything so low as stealing company secrets, let alone subjecting her, his own flesh and blood, to possible dismissal and criminal charges. He'd always been ambitious—sometimes she'd thought obsessively so—but never deceitful. Never as far as she could tell.

'It's highly confidential stuff so wait until the others have gone.' Again she remembered him instructing her that afternoon. 'And when you've finished, don't leave the information lying around . . . lock it safely away in your drawer and I'll collect it in the morning.' She recollected thinking how his concern for the firm's privacy was commendable. 'Oh . . . by the way,' he had added on that more cautious note, 'I'd appreciate it if you didn't mention this to Elliot . . . appreciate it if you didn't mention this to Elliot . . .'

Over and over David's words revolved around her brain, and the more she thought about them the guiltier they sounded, spinning round in a vortex of bewilderment and suspicion until she felt numb with hurt and fear. She wanted to get this whole thing sorted out. But if Elliot forced her to point a finger at her cousin and he was found to be doing something wrong—which was unlikely, she assured herself, but if he *was*—then she would not simply be admitting his negligence as she'd thought back at the office, but possibly sending him to prison . . .

She started as the car rocked violently. There was a loud, forceful thud as water was flung up by the wheels on her side, and she realised that only Elliot's razor-sharp reflexes when he had swerved had prevented them from coursing straight into the middle of the deep, black body of water on their side of the road. He was pulling into some sort of forecourt and with a nervous shudder Fleur realised that he was stopping the car. So this was it!

Wet cobbles gleamed under the Jaguar's powerful headlamps, and angry trees groaned heavily in the wind, their restless, swaying branches splintering the light from several Victorian-style lampposts, throwing eerie shadows across the stones. Puzzled, Fleur read the sign on the building opposite—'Cobblecourt Mews'—and an unbidden fear leapt through her. This wasn't the public house to which she had imagined he was taking her. This was his home! And all sorts of wild imagery started racing through her mind so that she shrank back as Elliot opened her door.

'No!'

'Oh yes.' It was a low growl as he reached in, pulling her forcefully out of the car. 'Did you imagine I'd make it any easier for you just because you're a woman?'

The determined set of his grim mouth had Fleur's dark eyes registering fear. She knew nothing about him. Only that he was unmarried. That he had been head of the Johannesburg office until taking over the chairmanship here in London, and that his total lack of sentiment in business extended to his private life—if those rumours she had heard were true—because it was said he was never seen with the same woman twice. So what chance was there for anyone he thought had wronged him? she reasoned, suddenly panicking, and with a small cry pulled away from him, only to slip on the wet cobbles in her high heels, so that she was huddled against the mews sign, grimacing from the pain of a twisted ankle as Elliot loomed above her.

'Look . . .' She swallowed to control the tremor in her

voice. 'I want to get this thing sorted out as much as you
do. I want to explain . . .' He was so close that she
stopped short, finding his nearness threatening.

'Then don't you think we'd be more comfortable
inside?' He tilted his head lightly towards the mews, his
voice surprisingly persuasive, so persuasive that Fleur
responded with the barest of nods. Though it wasn't
raining so hard now, the wind was cold, and she was glad
of the warmth which met them as they stepped through
the front door, although how she managed to reach it
without admitting to her injured ankle, she never knew.
Pride was the only thing which stopped her crying out in
pain.

The lounge was luxurious, thickly carpeted and graced
with two long, white leather settees. At the flick of a
switch a gas-burning log fire leapt into life between them,
the welcoming flames casting warm reflections on the
rug.

'Take off your coat and sit down.'

Fleur complied with Elliot's first command and when
he disappeared with the wet garment, dropped down on
to the soft, white leather of one of the settees. The smell
of fresh paint was apparent and vaguely her mind
registered that he must have started decorating as soon as
he had moved in. Two semi-circular windows with tiny,
individual panes were flanked by heavy, green curtains.
There was a bookcase against one wall, filled to capacity
with books, some rather expensive-looking hi-fi equipment and, adorning the wall opposite the fireplace, a
huge, abstract water-colour. She tried to make it out. It
looked like a sailing boat on top of triangles of
scaffolding, she thought, her nose wrinkling with
repugnance. If he liked *that* on his wall, what sort of
things went on in his mind?

'Obviously you find it as distasteful as I do.' She hadn't
realised he had returned and, caught unawares, coloured

profusely. 'Still, we aren't here to discuss the merits of art, are we? Here.' He tossed her a fluffy, white towel. 'Dry your hair.'

His own was unruly as if he had just rubbed it with a towel and raked it back into place with his hands, and nervously she noticed that he had removed his jacket and tie, the play of muscles beneath the fine quality shirt signifying strength, causing her throat to constrict painfully. She didn't know how she was going to begin to explain things to this hard, ruthless man. Whatever she said, she would be getting someone into trouble and whoever it was, she didn't imagine that Elliot would suffer them lightly. She didn't know what to do.

'Here.'

She looked up from drying her hair. He was holding out a glass containing a rich amber liquid. 'I-I don't drink . . . not spirits anyway,' she said, and was surprised by how much her voice shook.

'I rather think you need it.'

Of course. He could tell. And at his insistence she took the glass and gingerly sipped the liquor. It was probably his best cognac, she thought, but it tasted foul. Nevertheless, she continued to sip and felt its warming effects making her insides glow as it slid down.

'Now, Fleur . . .' Elliot perched himself on the arm of the settee, his own stretched across the back of it, in such close proximity to her that she could feel the warmth emanating from him, and she trembled. 'I think there was something you wanted to explain to me, wasn't there?'

She choked on the brandy, and went into a most unladylike fit of coughing. The glass was taken out of her hand and she sat back against the cushioning leather, drawing a few deep breaths. Her throat felt as if it were on fire.

'I need to make a phone call first,' she said

emphatically, brown eyes appealing to his.

Elliot tilted his chin in the direction of the telephone.

'In private?' she suggested, tentatively.

'Oh, no you don't!' There was harsh scepticism in his voice. 'And have you passing information on? What sort of bloody fool do you think I am?' He came to stand in front of her, long legs planted slightly apart. 'I want to know exactly how you got hold of Phoenix. What you were being paid for the information. And the name of the person who was paying you. And you'd better make it sooner rather than later, Fleur, because I'm running out of patience!'

That much was obvious. A muscle twitched spasmodically in his jaw and his hands were clenched at his sides. If I were a man he would have hit me by now, she thought numbly, trying to swallow her fear of him, although frustration was giving rise to a sudden rush of anger and before she knew it she was snapping back, 'I don't know anything, damn you! And I'm not trying to pass any information on! I couldn't care less about your stupid . . . Phoenix . . . I've already told you . . . I came by that password in complete innocence . . . I didn't know it was such a deadly secret! And I have to make a phone call because . . . well . . . because I have to, that's why!'

It was a feeble explanation and she knew it. But she had the strongest suspicion that if she told Elliot in his present mood just how she had got hold of Phoenix, he would be quite capable of killing his top sales executive.

'You'll tell me,' he seethed, dropping to his haunches in front of her, such a murderous glint in his eyes that for a moment she desperately wanted to. For her own sake.

'Are you working with anyone else?'

'No! I told you I . . .'

'Markham perhaps?'

'No!'

'He's your cousin, isn't he?'

'Yes, but . . .'

'Was that why you took the job in the first place? So that you could use that clever little brain of yours to ferret out information you could sell to our competitors?' He was on his feet again, pacing up and down in front of her, what had begun as a subtle inducement now a full-scale interrogation. 'Isn't that the truth of it?'

'No!' She was shaking under his condemning grey gaze—near to tears—and she didn't know what to say, what to do.

'This isn't the first time, is it?'

'I don't know what you mean.' She swallowed, her eyes wide, apprehensive, soft, blonde tendrils drying around her face.

'Don't you?' The man looked at her hard. 'I mean all the other projects which have been so inexplicably *leaked*. The contracts which have been lost over the past few months when we were just pipped at the post by our competitors. Did you think we weren't aware that something like this was going on?' He picked up a glass and poured himself a brandy, tossing it back in one gulp. 'It's time to come clean, Fleur.'

She sat, staring up at him, shaking her head. 'I don't know what you're talking about,' she answered, tremulously, and felt the sting of hot tears behind her eyes. Everything was wrong. What had seemed like a simple cover-up for negligence back at the office, now appeared to be every bit like something totally criminal, and in which David could be involved . . .

She shook away the thought, fighting back doubts. She couldn't let herself believe that. 'I don't know anything about that,' she uttered, miserably.

'Very well.' There was a threatening conclusiveness in those two words, and Fleur looked at him warily. 'Since you refuse to comply with me I'm afraid I have no alternative but to keep a close watch on you until the

Phoenix deal's completed, which at the least will be three, or even four days from now.' And when her eyes met his, questioning and hurt, he said simply, 'I can't let you leave here, Fleur.'

Horror-struck, she stared at him, fear pressing like a rock against her windpipe. You're crazy, she was about to say, and then thought better of it. Frank Steadman's indomitable heir might be hard, merciless even, but he was certainly in possession of all his faculties.

'That's abduction,' she whispered, a pulse beating furiously at her temple. 'You can get a prison sentence for that.'

'Maybe,' he grated, his breathing shallow, 'but don't imagine for one moment that Phoenix isn't worth that risk. It is.' He bent towards her, one hand on the arm of the settee, the other just above her shoulder imprisoning her there, and in hazy panic she noticed the full sensuality of that cruel mouth, the dark hairs curling over the unbuttoned neckline of his shirt, and she shrank back, sensing the determination in him. 'My father warned me while I was still in Johannesburg that something like this might be going on.' One of his hands was on her shoulder, pinning her back against the white leather, and she flinched from the bruising pressure of his fingers, the dangerous gleam in his eyes. 'A lot of people have put a lot of work into this project,' he breathed, the softness of his voice emphasising his anger, 'and I'll be damned if I'll let an unprincipled little brat like you screw the whole thing up.',

Apprehensive, Fleur clutched at the soft leather beneath her. Elliot looked brutal, his expression so inexorable that for a moment she almost blurted out the truth. But no, she couldn't! her better judgement clamoured, stopping her in time. Not until she had heard what David's part was in all this.

'Let me go,' she beseeched, and taking a deep breath

added with more courage, 'You've no power to keep me here against my will.'

Surprisingly, he relaxed his hold on her, his chest rising and falling heavily as he straightened.

'None, except for the fact that I'm stronger than you are.'

Fear shot through her again, making her pulses race. He'd use force? But yes, he would, she acknowledged, rubbing her shoulder where his hard fingers had bruised the soft skin. And probably in no uncertain terms, too!

'What about my job ... everyone at the office?' she ventured, shakily. 'Don't you think people will consider it odd if I don't show up for work?'

'*That*, my dear Miss Galaway,' he stated with cold formality, 'you should have thought of before you started playing around with things which didn't concern you.'

'My flatmate,' Fleur bluffed, thinking quickly, 'she'll ring the police if I don't come back tonight. I've never stayed out all night before.'

'Such virtue!' There was a cruel, derisory twist to the hard mouth. 'A pity your ethics don't extend to loyalty to your employer.'

'They do!' she shot back, trying to convince him. 'I haven't done anything wrong ...'

'And you don't have a flatmate either!' Elliot's tone was harsh. 'You rent accommodation in Finchley which you aren't sharing with anyone and I happen to know you're an orphan, so there won't be any interference there. A good try, my beautiful quarry, but it isn't going to work.'

He strode across to the drinks cabinet and Fleur stared after him with a feeling of impending doom. He wasn't stupid. He hadn't turned Steadman (Johannesburg) into one of the country's most prosperous companies without a considerable amount of insight, intellect and perception. Knowing him as she did, he had probably made it his business to vet everybody on his new payroll since he'd been in England, she thought, with a grimace, so she'd been utterly foolish thinking she could mislead him with a bluff like that. She felt worn out—totally defeated—and her ankle was beginning to throb.

'All right ... I'll admit I lied ... about having a flatmate I mean,' she confessed, subdued, to his broad back. 'But what makes you think you can possibly keep me here at all? Hasn't it occurred to you that while you're at the office I might just *try* and use the phone?'

Glass refilled, Elliot turned round, meeting her glittering challenge with an almost exasperated sigh. 'If you're so determined ...' He gestured towards her only hope of communication with her cousin. 'Be my guest.'

Did he really mean it ... at last? For a moment she couldn't move, sucking her lower lip as she considered what she could possibly say to David when she eventually got through. Well she would have to think about that when the time came, she decided, her ankle hurting so much that she found she could only hobble now to the other end of the room. But she would have to let him know of this awful predicament she was in. And also—somehow—find out who had instructed him to use that password, although that was going to be awkward, perhaps cause embarrassing repercussions for someone, with Elliot standing there.

Hand trembling, she lifted the receiver. And then stabbed frantically at the rest when she realised there was no dialling tone. But the mechanism failed to respond.

'You ...!' The word wouldn't come out. Angry, shaking with fear and frustration she looked up and saw the hard, grim lines of his face. He was moving towards her with a slow, easy assurance and in a blind panic she made a painful dart for the door. But even allowing for the time it took him to put down his glass, Elliot reached it first, so that she came to an abrupt and embarrassed halt against him.

'Oh no, my beautiful informant, you aren't going anywhere.' He was gripping her shoulders with such tenacity that she thought it was only his strength which was holding her up. Her ankle was hurting so much she didn't think she could have stayed vertical on her own. 'It's purely a lucky accident for me that the telephone people have been a bit lax with their reconnection,' he enlightened her with cool mockery, 'although in the circumstances I think we can delay it a little longer, don't you?'

She struggled violently, wincing as her right foot took most of her weight, and she felt Elliot's grip tighten, felt the strength in the unyielding wall of his chest as he held her against him. She could smell the potent, male scent of his skin beneath the fine, white shirt and fear raced through her veins like wildfire as she realised the impossibility of the situation, considered even that Elliot Steadman might well be a sexual pervert for all she knew, and a small choking sound escaped her.

'You can protest all you like.' His tone was implacable. 'You're staying here until the Phoenix contract is signed and sealed. And don't worry your pretty head that I'll try and rape you,' he surprised her with, as if reading her mind, 'because tempting though I might find your alluring body I'm rather particular about the women I sleep with. I tend to favour honesty and integrity over and above the probability of a good lay!'

Eyes blazing, Fleur tore herself fiercely away from him, flinching when a pain shot through her ankle like the stab of a knife. How dared he talk to her like that! As if she were some cheap tramp!

'You wouldn't recognise honesty and integrity if they jumped up and hit you in the face!' she spat back, the pale silk of her hair contrasting with the dark, dancing fire in her eyes. 'And if you don't let me go David will come looking for me. He comes to the flat regularly and he'll be the first to raise the alarm if he can't find me,' Which wasn't strictly true, she thought. David seldom called socially these days, but Elliot wasn't to know that.

A thick eyebrow lifted mockingly, black against the rich bronze of a Johannesburg tan. 'Let him.' There was a degree of almost sadistic relish behind his soft suggestion. 'But come hell or high water I'm not letting you out of here to ruin everything a lot of people have striven for ... *not until after the Phoenix deal's signed!*'

The stark finality with which he emphasised that last point assured Fleur that she was utterly trapped, and a resurgence of panic overwhelmed her. Fear lent her strength and she flew at him, nails extended, crying her protest in an angry, physical struggle, taking him by surprise, yet meeting an unassailable strength for which hers was no match. He was capturing her flailing arms with the minimum of effort, holding her under control while she sobbed out fresh protests, against the pain in her foot, his domination, and the dizzying sensation that every muscle of his hard body was suddenly burning through hers.

'For God's sake, Fleur ... put yourself in *my* shoes ... what other choice do I have?'

In a giddy, sickening daze she heard his last, exasperated words, felt the room spinning round and round, and all at once that warm, unconquerable strength seemed to be enveloping her. She seemed weightless, and from a long way off heard a voice say, '... better take a look at that ankle.' But then she knew only a gushing in her ears and she slipped into a deep, black void.

CHAPTER TWO

WHEN she opened her eyes she was lying on the settee and for a few moments couldn't remember where she was. Orange reflections were playing on the thick, creamy carpet and a pair of mud-splashed tights were lying in a crumpled heap nearby. And suddenly realisation dawned. They were *her* tights!

Swiftly she sat up. Elliot was sitting beside her, folding a clean, white handkerchief into a triangle over his knee.

'Feeling better now?' he queried, the barest hint of concern unable to conceal the underlying contempt in his voice.

Fleur blinked hard, still not quite able to comprehend what she was doing there, but when Elliot moved to place the makeshift bandage around her ankle, she remembered and pulled violently away from him.

'Don't you touch me!'

'I'm afraid it's a bit late for that.' Coolly, he caught the offending ankle and proceeded to bind it. 'You passed out on me and I had to make sure there was nothing fractured.'

'You ... you took off my tights,' she gulped, an embarrassed flush stealing across her cheeks.

'Don't worry ... it isn't a first experience for me,' he delivered, adding with biting sarcasm, 'but you were quite safe. I prefer my bedmates conscious, as well as principled.'

I'll bet you do! Fleur acknowledged silently, and felt a bush of hurt annoyance that he should doubt her own ethics. She watched how deftly he dealt with her swollen ankle, his hands cool and firm on her bare skin, a no

27

entirely unpleasant sensation, she forced herself to
admit. There were dark hairs on the backs of his hands,
black as that which fell across his forehead as he bent in
concentration, and her gaze ran over the high sweep of
his brow, the proud, straight nose and thrusting jaw, and
the flat, dark mole on his cheek. Some women would find
him very attractive, there was no doubt about that.

'Ouch!'

He had hurt her, deliberately, she felt, and gave him a
rebellious look as he slid up the settee towards her,
causing her to swallow hard. He was *close*!

'Just pray to your lucky stars that I don't hurt you as
much as I'm capable,' he recommended in a low voice,
'because at this particular moment I'm extremely
tempted to.'

And the next moment he swung away from her and
went out of the room.

Fleur leaned back against the soft leather and closed
her eyes, a deep sigh escaping her. Her employer thought
she was an industrial spy and because of it she was as
good as kidnapped. How on earth could a thing like this
have happened to *her*? And the crazy thing was she
couldn't see any way out of it. If she did manage to get
away from Elliot, perhaps went to the police, then in es-
tablishing her own innocence she would be ensuring an
investigation of David's. And if he was guilty...

Agitatedly, she sat up, her gaze meeting the horren-
dous-looking abstract on the opposite wall. It was about
as unpalatable as her thoughts. How could she imagine
David was guilty of anything? A hot flame of self-
reproach burned through her as she pictured him as he'd
been that day five years ago when he'd secured the job
with Steadman's—exuberant, bursting with enthusiasm.
It was just before she'd left home herself, she remembered, because he had come down to Cornwall to tell her
and Aunt Aggie, and they'd both been impressed that

he'd got such a responsible post while he was still only twenty-five. Over the past five years he'd seemed content, which was unusual for David, Fleur reflected, because he'd always had a restless nature, although recently that trait had seemed to surface at times. True he hadn't got that last promotion . . .

Elliot's return brought her swiftly back to the present. He was standing in front of her, hands planted firmly on his hips, his mouth set in a tight line. 'Now that you're feeling better I trust you've come to your senses and decided to give me an explanation for your actions this evening.'

His stance—of implacable resolve—was unnerving and Fleur cast her tongue over her lips. What was she supposed to say to him? 'David was the one who gave me that codename'? How could she until she had spoken to her cousin first?

'If you'd just let me out to make that phone call . . .' She stopped, realising that she was appealing to his retreating back, and with a sigh of hopeless despair she collapsed against the leather, her eyes closed. She wasn't sure how long she sat like that. She was only vaguely aware that Elliot was preparing something in the kitchen from the sounds and smells which touched her senses, and eventually he popped his head round the door to announce that dinner was ready.

'I'm not hungry,' she responded, and immediately her stomach grumbled loudly in protest. She didn't care if he had heard it or not. She was much too upset to eat, and though her stomach was craving food, she knew that if she did allow anything to pass her lips she would most probably be sick. Besides, there was no way that she wanted to share a meal with *him*. If he really thought she was guilty of something as underhand as he'd accused her of, then let him eat alone. The angry challenge of his gaze assured her he had read her thoughts perfectly, but he merely shrugged.

'Suit yourself. You'll eat ... when you're hungry enough.'

Alone again, Fleur listened to the sounds coming from the kitchen. The clink of cutlery against china, the sound of a glass being filled, evidence that reluctant guest or no, Elliot Steadman was allowing nothing to spoil the usual routine of his life—or his appetite. And a little later when he sat opposite her, totally relaxed and engrossed in a book, it became obvious to her that his nerves and endurance in this awkward situation were proving to be a lot stronger than hers. He was able to ignore her while all she could do was tug absently with the end of her watch-strap as she cast furtive glances around the large room, looking for a miraculous means of escape. Finally, she couldn't sit still any longer and, wincing painfully because her ankle was hurting so much, got to her feet and threw at him in a tight, rebellious voice, 'Since you're so determined to keep me here . . . you could at least have the courtesy to show me where I'm to sleep.'

Dark grey eyes met hers and an eyebrow lifted slightly. 'What makes you think you deserve that luxury?'

Nervously, Fleur gulped. What luxury was he referring to? His courtesy . . . or sleep? And if he meant the latter, was it in his plans then to try and withhold it from her? Her mind raced with the possibilities of how he might achieve that as she followed his silent figure to what was obviously his guest-room, the unmade double bed suggesting that this room hadn't yet been used.

As Elliot opened a cupboard, Fleur struggled to get a grip on her wild imagination. Elliot might be the epitome of ruthless masculinity, but he did have a high reputation to live up to, and that didn't include abducting young women for his own basic pleasure. Besides, a man like him wouldn't have to stoop to abduction, she admitted, somewhat reluctantly. He probably had women queuing at his door only waiting for a snap of his fingers to move in!

'Here.' He handed her a duvet, matching sheet and pillowcases, and she sank down on to the bed, needing to take the strain off her ankle. The mattress was soft and wide, but at that moment she would have given anything to have been curled up in her own, single divan.

'And what am I supposed to wear?' As soon as she said it she wished she hadn't. She noticed the derisory curl of Elliot's mouth, the cold gleam of mockery in his eyes.

'Such modesty.' He stood, staring down at her, making her feel uneasy. 'We must preserve that, mustn't we?'

Ignoring his sarcasm, Fleur watched him leave. Perhaps when he had gone to bed, she could try and find a way out of here, she thought hopefully, turning her attention to her surroundings. There were several packing cases bearing Johannesburg labels stacked against one wall, a reminder that her employer had only just moved into the mews, and she remembered then that he had been living in his late father's house since his arrival in this country. The gold carpet and curtains looked expensive—a rich contrast against the dark wood of the furniture—and the few small paintings on two of the walls were much pleasanter to look at than the monstrosity in the lounge. She wondered why he let it hang there when he obviously didn't like it, and then dismissed the thought. And noticing the semi-circular window, she limped over to it and looked out. It faced the cobbled courtyard as she'd supposed—she could see the trees bending heavily in the high wind—and she realised now that this building formed the end of a small terrace of similar ones. But it was the small brass object fastened to the window frame which brought her attention up sharply, and an attempt to open the window assured her of what she already feared. It was a lock, and it was doing a very effective job. She knew a ridiculous rush of panic, felt her throat go dry, and she backed away from the window cupping her hands over her nose and mouth and taking several deep, steadying breaths.

She had to keep calm. She'd had these moments of overpowering fear before and she'd handled them hadn't she?

'I trust you'll find this adequate for your requirements.' Elliot was offering her a black shirt—also a new toothbrush still in its packaging—and she took them both with a trembling hand. 'I'm sorry I can't offer you pyjamas but I never wear the things.'

Crazily, she blushed. The thought of his long, tanned physique lying totally naked in the next room to hers didn't serve to soothe her frayed nerves one little bit.

'Is anything wrong?' Obviously he had noticed the paling effects of her panic beneath the surge of colour.

'The window' she murmured, sickening fear, coupled with an uneasy sensual awareness, making her swallow hard. 'It's locked.'

'Of course it's locked,' he returned, calmly. 'The last couple to own this place were burgled twice and decided to take adequate steps to protect themselves. You'll find one on every window.'

Fleur stood up, running a slim hand under the platinum hair. 'Aren't you going to unlock it?' she asked, unsteadily, massaging the tight muscles of her neck.

'And let you get away?'

Of course. He couldn't risk that.

'Do you really think I'd jump from a first floor window?' she countered, acridly. 'I've already sprained one ankle.'

'It stays locked.' There was grim determination in his words.

'And supposing there's a fire? How the hell do I get out?' Her rising temper brought the grey eyes to the wild, amber flecks in her own.

'Wait until you see flames, then wake me up. Failing that . . . put a chair through the damn window!' He turned to go.

'You really think the worst of me, don't you?' Her soft accusation made him turn in the doorway, astonishment etching his dark, rugged features.

'That's a rather obvious statement of fact, isn't it?' he said coldly. 'I don't like deceit . . . of any sort . . . and I'd rather hoped you'd have been above something like that.'

Fleur opened her mouth to speak, and then dropped her gaze, totally unsettled by the cool deliberation of his. Had he given any thought to her then, before this unfortunate incident tonight? Was that what he was implying? The very idea led to an inexplicable quickening of her pulse.

'Won't you believe that I wasn't trying to pass any information on?' she tried again in a vain hope to convince him.

The cool, grey eyes appraised, narrowing as they took in the long, blonde hair, the slender neck and shoulders and the soft swell of feminine curves, rising and falling rather too quickly beneath the creamy wool, and Fleur touched her tongue to her lips, reading the unveiled desire in his gaze. In a second it was gone, replaced by that familiar condemnation as he shook his head.

'No,' he exhaled, strengthening his decision, and it was only after he had left her that she realised she was trembling from head to toe.

Sleep eluded her for hours. Any hope she was harbouring of trying to escape tonight ebbed slowly out of her when midnight chimed somewhere in the mews and Elliot still hadn't gone to his own room. She tossed and turned in the large bed, trying to forget that she was his prisoner, and that his shirt was like a sensual caress against her skin, but she couldn't stop worrying about David, about whether he could possibly be mixed up in trying to jeopardise a multi-million pound contract. Of course he couldn't, an inner voice kept trying to convince her, but the doubt still lingered, and she knew that only talking to David personally would put her mind at rest. But if there was still no telephone in the morning and she couldn't get out . . .

A door was closing softly in the room adjoining hers but slumber was already claiming her.

She was drifting inside a long dark tunnel, moving towards the light, looking for the way out, but at each end there was only glass. David was standing behind it with his back to her, and she kept hammering on the glass, hammering so hard that her knuckles hurt, but he didn't turn around. He was in danger and she had to make him hear her, but she couldn't get out of the tunnel, and he was starting to walk away!

David! She was screaming his name, watching his tall, blond figure slipping away from her—being drawn nearer and nearer to that unknown danger—and she couldn't get out to warn him because she was trapped . . .

No! *David*! *No*!

Someone was calling her name—shaking her urgently—and she struggled against a restraining hold until a sharp, stinging pain seared her cheek. She opened her eyes, shuddering and afraid, and for a moment didn't recognise the dark features hovering above her.

'For goodness sake, girl! Stop screaming! It's only a dream.' The deep, reasoning voice penetrated the depths of her nightmare, drawing her back to reality. 'What was that all about?'

Fleur took a few deep breaths, the curling tendrils of her blonde hair damp against her cheek. 'It . . . was only a dream,' she accepted, her voice shaking, partly because of the horror of it, partly because Elliot was rather too close for comfort.

'Some dream,' he stated, grimly.

Through the undrawn curtains a shaft of light from an autumn moon fell like a pale shroud across the bed, illuminating the soft green of the duvet. In the half light, Elliot's strong profile stood out in sharp relief—the high, chiselled forehead, the long, patrician nose, the slim line of his upper lip above the fuller, cruel curve of the lower. He was wearing only a short, dark towelling robe which exposed his strong, muscular legs and most of his chest where it gaped and Fleur realised a dangerous sexual awareness when he moved to lightly touch her shoulder.

'You're hot . . . trembling. Can I get you something?'

She nodded, unable to find her voice, her body tingling with peculiar sensations. 'A drink of water,' she managed to get out eventually.

He came back with some fresh orange juice which was even better, sitting down on the edge of the bed while she sipped it.

'What were you dreaming that frightened you so much?' he asked, when she had had enough of the juice.

'It was . . . nothing worth talking about,' she answered hesitantly, setting aside the glass on the bedside table. She didn't want to discuss it with him.

'That wasn't how it sounded to me. You were screaming for Markham.' He looked at her obliquely, his eyes steely cold. 'Just what sort of a relationship do you have with that man?'

'He's my cousin,' she returned sharply, disliking the inference in Elliot's tone.

'Oh come on . . . he's more than that, isn't he?' he suggested, censoriously.

Yes, he is, she thought. Much more. But if you think I'm explaining that to you, you got another think coming.

'It's none of your business,' she retorted instead. And winced as strong hands slid under her, pulling her close to that threateningly male body.

'I think it is my business,' he said, his voice a low

warning. 'Because if you've been scheming together on this Phoenix deal I want to know about it . . . now!'

'No, we . . . we haven't,' she defended, meekly, daunted by the harshness of his voice, the bruising pressure of his fingers and the close proximity in which she found herself to him. She could smell the masculine scent of his body—potent and disturbing—mingling with the last traces of his cologne.

'I can be quite unscrupulous, Fleur.' His whisper was a sensual threat, and she gasped as he jerked her closer to him so that her back was arched, causing the black shirt to fall open where it had been carelessly fastened, leaving very little of her high, young breasts concealed. 'After all . . . you've very few scruples yourself, have you?'

Tense, rigid, she felt his warm breath fan her skin—wanted to push him away, yet was held in the grip of some mesmeric influence which rendered her helpless and still. But when his tongue flicked lightly against the silken valley of her breasts, self-preservation surfaced and she pressed her hands hard against the coarse hair of his chest, using all her energies to try and free herself.

'No!'

Her strength was ineffectual against his. He wouldn't let her go! Primitive sensations were contesting with a heightening rush of panic. He could take her if he wanted to, and there was nothing she could do to stop him!

But the next moment she was lying breathless, flung back against the pillows, and Elliot was getting to his feet.

'You traitorous little bitch!' Through the darkness she caught his oath of self-condemnation. Though he sounded as breathless as she was. 'Get some sleep,' he recommended more steadily 'or we'll both be guilty today' of taking without consent.'

She listened to his footsteps retreating along the passageway, hating herself for that initial spark which

had leaped in her at his touch. He was holding her here
against her will. No amount of physical attraction could
cloud the reality of that. She had to think of a way to try
and get out of here, get to David so that she could prove
his innocence—and her own. She thought about the
dream in which he had figured—the screams which had
brought Elliot to her room—and knew it had stemmed
from the feeling of being trapped. That familiar,
gripping fear which even now was making her break out
in a cold sweat.

Sitting up, she took several sips of the orange juice and
slid down under the duvet with a deep, disconsolate sigh.
As if she didn't have enough on her plate already, she
thought, wretchedly. Now the nightmares had started all
over again.

The briefs and tights which she had washed in the
bathroom sink had dried well overnight on the heated
towel-rail, and she put them on, together with her creamy
wool dress. She didn't feel her best, wearing yesterday's
clothes, but then she didn't look it either, she thought,
catching sight of herself in the bathroom mirror. She
hadn't slept well after that dream so that she looked pale
and washed out. There were dark circles under her eyes
and her hair was in dire need of washing and styling, the
heavy silk falling in wild disarray around her shoulders.
She'd intended to do that when she'd got home last night,
she remembered, and suddenly wondered what David
would think today when he went into the office and
found that she wasn't there. Would Elliot phone in and
make some excuse for her? Or would he simply leave
everyone wondering why she hadn't turned up? And
supposing David went round to the flat and found it
empty? He was expecting that information from her
about Phoenix this morning, she ruminated, her stomach
churning sickeningly as she fastened the small, pearly

buttons at her throat. What would he do if he couldn't
find her? Ring the police? Perhaps he would, she
thought, wistfully, her anxious gaze running along the
shelf with its hairbrush, electric shaver and bottle of
masculine cologne, because although she didn't always
see eye to eye with David these days, he still knew her
well enough to know that there wasn't anyone in her life
now important enough to make her want to stay away
from the flat—spend the night with them.

'You look like death.'

Elliot's unflattering remark did little to help the way
she felt as she limped into the kitchen. As usual he looked
immaculate. Clean-shaven, his sleek, dark hair still
damp from the shower, he exuded a freshness that
blended with the unexpected sunshine of the morning.
He was casually dressed in dark blue cords and a white,
polo-necked sweater and looked so different from the
usual, thrusting executive Fleur was used to seeing, that
for a few moments she couldn't take her eyes away from
him.

'Even the Chairman of the Board is granted a few days
off for moving house,' he said, coolly, answering her
unspoken question, and uneasy, she turned away,
disconcerted by how perfectly he had read her thoughts.
'Bacon and eggs?'

Her stomach churned nauseously again. How could
she be so hungry and yet feel so sick? 'No thanks . . . just
coffee.'

It was obvious from the empty dishes on the table that
Elliot had already eaten, and Fleur sat down with the cup
of coffee he handed to her, adding milk and sugar from
the bowl and jug. The beverage was hot and delicious
—freshly percolated—and was just what her empty
stomach craved.

'How's the ankle?' Elliot cast a dispassionate glance
down at her foot.

'Better, thanks,' she replied in a clipped voice, her politeness as forced as his. It was still very painful though, but she had removed the makeshift bandage and now she pushed it across the table to where he stood, gathering up the empty dishes, saying, 'I don't think I need this any more.'

He pocketed the handkerchief without a word, and depositing the dishes in the sink, turned back to her. 'I'm sorry I had to slap you last night.'

Fleur glanced up, puzzled. She wasn't aware that he had.

'When you were screaming,' he enlightened her, answering her silent query. 'Much as you deserve it, I don't normally go in for beating women. It was the only way I could wake you before you roused the whole damn court.'

The memory of her horrendous nightmare came vividly to her mind and she flinched as she sipped the warming coffee, aware that Elliot was looking at her intently, taking in the pallor of her cheeks, no doubt, and her lacklustre eyes.

'You'd better eat something.'

'I'm not hungry,' she answered, staring into her cup.

She heard the chair opposite hers being dragged out and he sat down, forcing her by will alone to meet his eyes. They were flickering with hot anger as he said, 'If you think that going on a hunger-strike is going to make me change my decision in any way, then you'd better get it straight right now. It won't.' There was stark finality in his words. 'There'll be no reprieve, Fleur.'

His grey gaze held hers for a long moment during which she sensed his determination like shock waves in the air between them. Those dark, rugged features were rigid with purpose, and apprehensively she realised that this was no ordinary man whom she'd so innocently crossed, but a forceful tower of granite who wouldn't bend or break under the pleas of that innocence. So she resolved not to humiliate herself by offering them.

'You can't keep me here,' she assured him, trying to sound confident.

And he answered, 'No?'

Half-rebelliously, her gaze followed his tall, lithe physique as he strode over to the sink and began running the taps, and in spite of herself Fleur couldn't help thinking how capable he was—needing no one, not even in his home—the simple domestic task of washing-up taking nothing away from that hard, impregnable masculinity.

'David will send for the police. They'll come looking for me,' she promised vehemently, but he ignored her, placing the last dish he had washed with the others to dry.

'I'm going out,' he said then to her utter surprise, and drying his hands added, with a cold derision, 'I'll try not to be *too* long.'

She was relieved when he went, watching from the window as the Jaguar started up with a powerful growl, nibbling her lower lip. Now was her chance to try and get away!

Minutes later she realised that he hadn't been joking when he had said there were locks on all the windows. The front door was locked, too, from the outside, and trying the telephone again she found that it still wasn't working. Wretchedly, she limped back into the small, oak-furnished kitchen, and washed up her own cup and saucer. And then for something to do began drying the dishes which Elliot had washed and left to drain, chewing over the nagging suspicion which had been troubling her since last night.

Was David guilty of trying to jeopardise the Phoenix contract? He couldn't be! she thought, agonisingly, opening several drawers until she found the one where

the cutlery belonged. But unhappily her mind wandered
to the resentment which had been simmering in her
cousin since Elliot had taken over the chairmanship of
Steadman's and appointed Andrew Moreton as his right-
hand man. Andrew, whom everyone had thought had
been the lucky one because of his seniority, his
experience, his quiet, unruffled approach to top-level
problems. Everyone had said that if Frank Steadman
had been alive, David would have got the job. But Frank
had died. And Elliot was ruling the empire. And that
promotion David had hoped for had never
materialised . . .

A shrill, tuneful whistling acted like a guillotine on
Fleur's troubled thoughts. There was someone outside!

Racing through into the lounge and peering eagerly
out of the window, she looked right and left, but could see
no one at first. The trees across the road flanked a park,
she noticed now, and the high winds had dropped,
leaving their sparse leaves silent and still. Large puddles
from last night's rain reflected the sunlight like mirrors
placed at random amongst the cobblestones, and Fleur
blinked hard, her eyes dazzled by the brightness of the
autumn morning.

And then the sound came again. This time ac-
companied by a rattling of bottles, and from the end of
the mews buildings a milk wagon moved into view. It
stopped and a man clambered out, delivering to the
adjoining house, and without thinking, Fleur hammered
hard on the pane, trying to catch his attention as he
strode back to the wagon. She wasn't sure what she
expected him to do, but he was contact with the outside
world! But damn the man! He was making so much noise
with his bottles and his whistling that he couldn't hear
her!

She shook the curtain violently, and it worked. The
whistling stopped and he looked up. Frantically, she

waved. Saw the man raise a hand in acknowledgement before he started swinging his crate towards Elliot's front door, and without a thought for her ankle Fleur dashed across the lounge and out into the hall, plans of how she might send a message through him to David still not clear in her mind. She heard the thud as a bottle was placed on the doorstep. Heard the whistling start up again. But by the time she flung herself against the heavy door, the sound was dying away. She called through the brass letter-box to try to bring the man back, but the slow whine of the wagon pulling out of the mews was her only answer.

Anguished, defeated, she slumped down on to the bottom stair, tears of frustration scalding her eyes. He'd thought she was reminding him to leave a pint of milk! Oh what cruel joke was fate playing on her? She didn't want to do anything to hurt David—jeopardise his job—and yet if she didn't say anything to Elliot, she could well be helping someone, perhaps even David, get away with gross malpractice against the company, she thought, shuddering. She was torn—utterly torn—between loyalty and love for her cousin, and a cold, perhaps incriminating duty to Elliot, and she didn't know which way to turn. If she could only get to David. Hear it from his own lips that he wasn't involved in anything wrong, then he could tell Elliot that she wasn't involved either.

A long time later she hobbled upstairs to the bathroom. The pain in her ankle felt worse from her reckless dash to the front door and her eyes, when she looked in the mirror, stared back at her, red-rimmed, mascara-streaked. Quickly she splashed cold water on to her cheeks. Creamed the black streaks from under her eyes and applied fresh mascara and lipstick. Whatever happened she wouldn't let Elliot see that she had been crying. He'd probably take it as a symptom of guilt!

As she was brushing the heavy, blonde hair, she suddenly noticed that the lock securing the frosted-glass window was unlike any of the others in the building. It was secured with two visible screws, she discovered, on closer inspection, so that anyone with a screwdriver . . .

A *screwdriver*!

With lightning speed she darted straight towards the kitchen, gasping when her ankle protested at the sudden burst of activity, but it didn't deter her. She'd seen a screwdriver in the drawer where Elliot kept the cutlery!

In seconds she was back at the window, using all her strength to turn the screws which refused to budge at first, but then slowly started to turn. With trembling hands she removed the lock and pushed open the window, wondering desperately if she did manage to call to someone, what on earth she would say. That she'd accidentally locked herself in? That the handle had come off the bathroom door perhaps, and could they possibly get a ladder?

And then her heart jumped wildly. There was no point in calling anyone! She was at the rear of the building and a small wing of the lower storey jutted out under the bathroom window. Probably a laundry room, or a cellar, she guessed, behind the garage under the living quarters, but the roof-level was flat, and would only take a small jump to reach from here.

Without wasting any time she fetched her handbag from the bedroom, donned her trench coat and, heart thumping from the prospect of Elliot coming back and catching her, swung her legs over the sill.

His garden was long, like a wild, unruly jungle, but she could see a lane running alongside it, as she made for the edge of the low roof and started to lower herself over the side. The rough stonework made a good foothold, although it did very little for her patent leather shoes. Her ankle throbbed miserably, and she knew she had snagged her tights. Still, she was past caring, she decided, just so long as she could get away. And a moment later she was easing herself over the fence into the lane, and she was free.

CHAPTER THREE

'COULD you tell me where I could find a telephone, please?'

The man in the park paused from sweeping up the leaves and was looking her up and down with some amusement. It probably wasn't every day that he was approached by some breathless, limping female with a hole in her tights, Fleur thought wryly.

'Go over to the main gate . . .' The park attendant leaned on his broom to direct her, and thanking him as if he had just offered her the crown jewels, she tore away, her heart racing with anticipation.

What would David say to her? What reason would he give her for wanting that confidential data on Phoenix? Desperately she needed—yet half dreaded—to know the answer.

She had nearly reached the main gate. The man had said there was a call-box just outside, she remembered, coming into an avenue of trees. Only a few more minutes and her troubles could be over. Well, her immediate ones, anyway, she thought, with a dull ache in the pit of her stomach, because if David was guilty . . .

Out of breath, praying fervently that she had enough loose change for the phone, a strange tingling down her spine made her glance back, and suddenly her heart came up into her mouth. Elliot was behind! And from the speed at which he was moving he had every likelihood of catching her.

She started to run for all she was worth, her ankle hurting badly, but she didn't care if the swelling came up again like a balloon. She had to reach the phone! But

Elliot's footsteps were coming closer, his breathing hard
and relentless, and as he made a grab for her, she let out a
small cry of defeat. His fingers were bruising with their
grip of iron, and she was struggling against it with all the
energies she had left in her body, her fists pummelling
the solid wall of his chest in a futile bid for freedom.

'Let me go! Let me go!'

'And let you ruin everything Phoenix stands for?' He
was breathless himself, his features as hard and
unyielding as his chest through the brown leather jacket.
'Is that where you were going? To trade secrets with your
confederates!'

'No!' She twisted violently in his grasp, but he didn't
relax it, merely pulled her more into the cover of the trees
so that they weren't on view to anyone who happened to
pass by.

'I ought to break your precious little neck . . .'

'Go on then!' Despite the menace of Elliot's tone,
anger sparked in Fleur's eyes, lending her courage to
stand up to the fury she read in his. 'What you're doing is
more low-down and unscrupulous than anything you
think I'm supposed to have done!' she spat at him. 'And
if you don't let me go this minute . . . I'll make a scene!
You couldn't stand a scene, could you, Elliot?' Above the
drumming pulse in her temples, her words came out as a
cool, deliberate taunt, and nervously she licked her lips,
wondering where she was finding the pluck to challenge
him like this. 'Your clients might not be too inclined to
sign that contract if they read tomorrow's papers and see
that the Chairman stooped to abduction because he
couldn't stand the competition!'

She didn't stop to think how far she was going. How
her words could well be taken as an admission of guilt,
and she saw the sudden tensing of Elliot's jaw, but at that
moment didn't care. All she was alive to was the sound of
voices which were drawing nearer and her gaze flew

towards the two men approaching along the path. If she
screamed now, they would hear her! she thought
recklessly. But in the same instant Elliot seemed to read
what was in her mind.

Too quick for her, he forced her back against a tree,
suppressing the fight she would have put up against him
by holding her arms firmly behind her back, while his
mouth descended on hers. She tried to protest. Tried
writhing to draw attention to herself, but his body was
crushing hers so that she couldn't move, and his mouth
was bruising in its purpose. She heard one of the men
make some earthy comment as he passed. Thought
wildly how she and Elliot must look. Like desperate
lovers, she guessed. And realised humiliatingly that that
was precisely the impression he wanted to give.

His punishing kiss seemed to go on and on, stifling her
groans of objection, until she felt dizzy, robbed of breath,
her legs threatening to buckle under her. And suddenly
she wasn't resisting any longer. She wasn't sure at what
point she actually stopped, only aware that his arms had
tightened painfully around her, leaving hers free, and she
was accepting his harsh invasion of her mouth, clinging
to the leather jacket for support as every nerve cell in her
body awakened to a dangerous, throbbing excitement.
But then he was setting her back against the tree,
glancing past her with a cool casualness, checking, no
doubt, that they were alone again.

'Bastard.' It came out as a trembling whisper, and
Elliot's mouth twisted mockingly.

'You'd do well to remember it,' he breathed, softly
threatening, one hand coming up to rest just above her
shoulder. 'I'm not a man to be messed with as you're
going the right way to finding out.'

A cold globule from last night's rain dropped from a
leaf and splashed against her cheek, and she shivered.
'And I suppose you think you can just go ahead and drag

me back with you, do you, you big bully?' Her mouth
tightened in a mutinous line, although her heart was
thumping so hard she thought Elliot must surely be able
to hear it. 'How do you know it isn't too late? What
makes you so sure I haven't been to one of your
neighbour's houses . . . told them all about you?'

A muscle moved in the strong, jutting jaw. 'Apart from
the fact that there appeared to be no one in when I went
out . . . or came back . . . I think you're far too
independent-minded for that. You'd rather sort things
out yourself than go running to the first available source
of help. According to office records your initiative and
ingenuity fall into the "A" category, along with regular
attendance and . . . honesty.' His tone ridiculed. 'So . . .
Miss Virtue,' he said slowly, precisely, 'you're going to
walk back with me now without a murmur and you're not
going to think about running off again.'

Platinum hair falling over one shoulder, Fleur held his
gaze challengingly. 'And if I don't go along with your
plans?' she enquired, brittly.

'You will.'

A startled blackbird shot out of a tree overhead,
protesting loudly, the cold droplets sent down by its
agitated wings making her shudder almost as much as
Elliot's grim resolution.

'Because if you don't . . .' he straightened, his eyes as
hard as grey marble, 'I'll make it my business to see that
neither you, nor your precious *David*, ever works in a
position of trust again.'

She looked at him, at the cold eyes and hard mouth,
her gaze going unwittingly over the waisted jacket to the
cord-clad legs which were planted slightly apart, standing firm, defying challenge, and she swallowed. He
meant every word he said. He could ruin both her and
David—he had the power to do it—and to antagonise
him now might perhaps result in his taking strong

measures against David's recent laxity, especially if he were also found to have broken a board member's trust in giving her that password. Or worse . . .

She shuddered again, turning away from him. To comply seemed the only thing to do.

The pain from her ankle was almost unbearable by the time Elliot let her into the mews. All the way back a raging pride had forced her to try to walk normally beside his grim, silent figure. She'd been determined that he wouldn't guess at how much pain she was in. But now the agony, coupled with a lack of food and sleep, brought on a sudden nausea as she reached the lounge and she grabbed at the door-jamb, bending low to alleviate the sickness which was washing over her in waves.

'What the . . .' She heard his soft expletive as he moved to steady her—lift her—and she took an absurd comfort from his arms as he carried her to the settee.

'We'll have an end to this,' he promised with a quiet firmness as she flopped back against the leather, the nausea starting to subside. 'You're going to eat something if I have to tie you down and force feed you. Is that clear?'

Of course. He knew exactly what was wrong with her. And she nodded, too weak and emotionally spent to argue.

Early that evening Fleur emerged from the bathroom draped in a white, fluffy towel, her hair falling from a side plait over one shoulder. Her body felt luxuriously bathed and soothed, her bare feet revelling in the deep warmth of the carpet, and already she was feeling stronger again after the steamed fish and beautifully-cooked vegetables Elliot had insisted she eat.

He was sitting with one arm stretched across the back of the settee, listening to a record—something by Mozart which she recognised. She remembered him saying

casually once at the office that he liked Mozart—
remembered how, laughingly, she'd complimented him
upon his taste. But she forgot about the music because he
looked up as she came into the lounge, and something
leaped in his eyes, something fierce and consuming, so
that she felt the colour spread across her cheeks from the
gaze that raked unashamedly over her semi-nakedness.

'I haven't anything clean to put on,' she said in a
barbed voice, striving for composure under the heat of
those assessing eyes. 'Have you considered what I'm
supposed to wear if I'm expected to stay here for the next
three days?'

He stood up and moved towards her with the grace of a
wild and beautiful animal, a twist of a smile on his lips.

'I see nourishment's helped to put back the sharp edge
to your tongue. That's a good sign.' He grimaced. 'I was
beginning to fear I had a total invalid on my hands.'

'Don't worry . . . you haven't quite broken me yet,' she
threw back, although it was difficult keeping her voice
steady when his gaze seemed to be removing the towel
from around her slender body.

A soft, involuntary gasp escaped her as his hands came
to rest behind her shoulders, giving rise to a strange
tingling along her spine. She felt totally exposed, Elliot's
febrile eyes seeming to strip her not only of her wrap, but
of her resistance to him.

'Had it occurred to you, my lovely traitress, that if I
keep you naked . . .' Insolently, his finger traced a line to
the tantalising division between her breasts. 'You won't
be so inclined to run away?'

She wanted to tug away from him, but unfamiliar
sensations held her in thrall, sensations which were
basically primitive and bore no relation to liking or
respect. She despised him for keeping her here—hated
him, if that wasn't too strong a word—and yet his dark
attraction was electrifying to her physical make-up, and

beneath the towel she felt the eager response of her breasts.

'Why . . . why don't you just hand me over to the police?' Tensely, her tongue flicked over her lips and Elliot's gaze followed the nervous gesture, noting the sensuality behind it. 'Why don't you?' she repeated, a tremor in her voice.

His hands moved smoothly along her arms, caressing, but with a purposeful strength behind their gentleness. 'Perhaps I want my pound of flesh,' was his soft, taunting reply.

Fleur lifted a finely arched eyebrow, pulse thudding as she sneered, 'Literally?'

He gave a soft laugh. 'And mar that beautiful body? Oh no.' He shook his head, appraising her. 'I'll take you intact.'

His words registering their true meaning, Fleur pulled back from him, the gentle music playing through the stereo inconsistent with the rapid drumming of her heart.

'Shocked?' he queried, with some ridicule. 'I can't think why.' Through a heady daze his voice came to her with a flaying edge. 'After all . . . you know as much as anyone about taking, don't you, Fleur?'

Her brown eyes appealed to the murky depths of his. 'I didn't . . .' she protested, but he didn't let her finish.

'And lying about it!'

His voice grazed with the efficiency of hard gravel and for a moment he looked every bit as if he might reach for her and deal out some very rough treatment. But suddenly he swung away from her as if he were tired of their conversation—as though he couldn't bear to look at her any longer—and Fleur exhaled quiet relief.

'You'll find something in the cupboard.' He gestured impatiently towards the spare bedroom. 'I'm sure that with your contriving little brain you'll be able to team *something* up.'

His sarcasm flayed her. He must think me the lowest of the low, she thought, going through into the bedroom. And really, when she gave enough consideration to it—forgot about her own anger—who could blame him, when she hadn't offered him any explanation for being in possession of that password? He'd ridiculed the firm's opinion of her openness, too, she remembered, feeling the fresh sting of his derisory attitude towards her in the park. And that hurt most of all. She'd never committed a dishonest deed in her life, she thought, ironically, throwing open the cupboard door. Not consciously, anyway . . .

There was sportswear, and a couple of squash racquets in the cupboard—evidence of how Elliot kept fit—plus a number of shirts, one of which she teamed with a pair of paint-spattered dungarees. They belonged to someone shorter than herself, she decided, wonderingly, because the bib didn't reach as far up as it should have, and she had to adjust the straps, and since she had washed her underwear and left it over the heated towel-rail again to dry, the soft outline of her breasts was clearly visible through the semi-transparent shirt. Still, there was nothing else to put on, she thought, grimacing at her reflection in the mirror, and wondered what Elliot would think. When she found out it was too late to change back into her dress.

'Is this another of your softening tactics?'

The accusation in his voice made her look up. Sitting opposite her, his eyes were glinting like steel as they rested on the soft swell of her breasts, and inevitably she blushed.

'What do you mean?' she queried, swallowing.

His mouth moved wryly as his eyes met hers. 'First a hunger-strike. Now a get-up that looks like something out of *Playboy*.' He snapped shut the book he had been absorbed in. 'If seduction's in your plans . . . forget it! It won't work.'

Fleur's colour heightened, her lips tightening before she exhaled vehemently, 'You flatter yourself! I wouldn't try and seduce you if you were the last man on earth! There weren't any thicker shirts in that cupboard . . . and it isn't my fault if I haven't got anything else to wear while my underwear's drying! And by the way you keep stressing how immune you are to me, I'm beginning to think you're frightened that really you aren't!'

She shrank back as Elliot sprang to his feet, and she caught her breath, unconsciously gripping the soft, white leather with tense fingers. But he swung away from her, across the room, and she began to breathe again.

What on earth had possessed her to say a thing like that to him? she thought, incredulously. After that little episode in the park today, if anyone's defences were in danger of slipping they were hers, not his.

'Do you want a drink?'

His question caught her slightly off-balance. She hadn't expected that.

'Do you have an orange juice?'

The hard mouth quirked at the corner. 'Nothing stronger?'

'I told you,' she answered, tremulously, the way he was looking at her, so reflectively, suddenly making her nervous. 'I don't drink. Only white wine,' she went on to clarify. 'And then only ever one glass with a meal.'

Elliot shrugged and turned back to the drinks cabinet, leaving her wondering why she had even bothered to tell him that much. He'd hardly be interested in her private life.

Absently her hand slid into the pocket of the dungarees, closing around a small, cold object, and curiously she drew it out, staring down at it in surprise. It was an earring—a small reproduction of a delicate, pink

flower. But quickly she replaced the tantalising find as
Elliot handed her the glass of juice, and she gasped,
flinching when his fingers twisted around the gold rope
of her hair, forcing her startled eyes to meet the grey
antagonism of his.

'Let's get one thing straight, my beautiful temptress,'
he advised, in a voice ragged with contempt. 'Nothing
would give me greater satisfaction at this moment than to
drag you into bed and make you beg clemency for that
little remark just now. So if you want a taste of my real
anger . . . just carry on the way you're going!'

Fleur looked away from him, her lashes fluttering
nervously against the smooth satin of her cheeks. She
was playing with fire—taunting a man like Elliot. She
could feel his dark, brooding anger burning against her
now like a searing torch, yet in spite of it couldn't stop
herself retaliating, 'Do you always get the better of your
women with brute force?'

A small protest left her as he clasped her chin with a
sure roughness, although the touch of his thumb as it
brushed across her lips was light—sensual—sending a
betraying little tingle down her spine.

'You're hardly one of my women, are you?' he assured
her, cuttingly. 'Do you really think I *want* you here?'

No, Fleur thought, without any shred of doubt as she
watched him stride away from her. I'm probably
cramping his style! And wondered, with a raging
curiosity, what the woman who owned the earring was
like. Slim, but more petite than herself, if those
dungarees were anything to go by, she ruminated, her
mind conjuring up a picture of a very sophisticated
brunette. She imagined Elliot would like brunettes.
Especially the type who were prepared to help him
decorate. And judging by the colour of the paint on the
dungarees she was wearing, this one had had a very free
hand with the lounge.

Had she slept here? she wondered, staring at the flames leaping around the simulated logs in the grate. And if so, where? In Elliot's bed? After all, the one in the spare room hadn't been made up last night.

She couldn't put a name to the surge of hot emotion which coursed through her, and hearing the squeak of leather looked up to see Elliot taking up his book again, a crystal glass containing neat Scotch on the small table beside him. He was doing his best to ignore her again, she realised, somewhat nettled, but couldn't stop herself from stuyding him while his eyes were averted.

His hair wasn't completely black, as she'd always assumed, but showed hints of red under the light. Sign of a fiery temper, she thought with a mental grimace, because it certainly applied to the man sitting opposite her. His eyelashes were black, though—black and thick and long—casting feathery shadows on his cheeks while he read, his cruel, sensual mouth hinting at a passion far more explosive and fiery than that of any anger.

Yes, definitely in Elliot's bed, she decided, her thoughts going back to the brunette. He was too virile— too male—to bother with a woman who wouldn't be prepared to satisfy his basic needs. And a small frisson went through her as she considered that, given the right circumstances, a woman could probably be driven to ecstasy in that powerful embrace . . .

'Have I suddenly sprouted horns or something?'

His soft mockery shamed her into realising that she had been enjoying a delightful, visual tour of his marvellous physique without any reservation whatso-ever, and she looked away, totally disconcerted.

'Let me go home,' she appealed, tilting her face to his again.

'No,' he answered, bluntly, and then more softly, but with no less determination, 'not until contracts are signed on Phoenix.'

His book discarded, he leaned forward, giving her his sole attention with blatant contempt. 'My father killed himself over this project—literally!—worked himself to death—and I'll take every step in my power to prevent anyone lousing up all he spent months—years!—striving for.' There was a tautness to the strong jaw which made Fleur shudder as he said, with unrelenting purpose, 'Even if it means winding up behind bars!'

She was clutching her glass so tightly it was in danger of shattering and so she put it down, fiddling nervously with her watchstrap as she met the cold rigidity of his gaze. There were tiny creases around his eyes that she hadn't really noticed before—dark shadows beneath them—and suddenly she was acutely sensitised to a depth of emotion which surprised her—an immense agony of loss beneath that hard, masculine shell. He'd been an only child, she knew that much, knew also that Frank Steadman had been widowed for more than thirty years. So father and son must have been unusually close, she thought, considering her own background—the aunt who had been mother, father and friend all rolled into one.

'I'm sorry,' she murmured, her throat constricting, for the first time beginning to appreciate his motives.

'Are you?' His words cut into her like broken glass, and the grey eyes accused.

Of course. He suspected *her* of trying to ruin all Frank Steadman had worked for. 'Yes,' she managed to say with the strength of her sincerity. 'I liked him.'

Elliot's lips compressed, but he said nothing, picking up his drink and disposing of it in one gulp. She wondered what he was thinking. Perhaps of the kindly, grey-haired man who was tough but compassionate, and who had died so suddenly two months ago. A heart attack caused through stress, someone had said.

Numbly, Fleur stared up at the watercolour with its

conglomeration of triangles and its colourless-green wash, considering how much truth had lain behind that casual remark. Had Frank Steadman been worrying about leaks in his company's security? Was that what had helped send him to his grave? Had someone, perhaps David . . .

She shut her mind against that unthinkable suspicion, suddenly feeling sick and, uttering an inaudible excuse to Elliot, took herself off to bed despite the early hour, tired out from the emotions of the past days. But she couldn't sleep for worrying about David—about how he had got hold of that password and what he had been planning to do with the information to which it gave him access. Suspicion had been born in her mind and she couldn't let it go, torn between whether or not she should mention it to Elliot, yet shying away from any betrayal of her own flesh and blood. He had to be innocent, she thought, feverishly, and it would only take one telephone call to allay these awful suspicions . . .

She tossed restlessly in sleep, beads of perspiration breaking out on her upper lip as her head moved wildly from side to side. She was trapped again inside that glass tube, panicking, banging hard on the thick, immovable wall of glass until her knuckles were bruised. Crying, choking, gasping for air. She thought her lungs would burst from screaming, terror rising upon terror because nobody would come.

And then she was sobbing and gasping, sitting up in bed and clinging to a warm, firm substance that was comforting and reassuring, calming her with deep, soothing words in the lonely darkness of the night.

'It's all right! You were dreaming again. It's all right.' Elliot's voice was firm and very real, acting like a tranquilliser on her frayed nerves. 'You were screaming so loudly I thought you were being murdered.' And more gently, 'Want to tell me about it?'

She didn't, she thought, shuddering. She didn't even
want to think about it. But Elliot's arms were warm and
strong around her, and she was suddenly conscious of the
fact that her face was pressed against the coarse hair of
his chest, exposed by the gaping rope. She could hear the
strong, steady beat of his heart—at variance with the
wild hammering of her own—and in a half daze noticed
the pleasant, slightly musky scent of his skin.

'I was trapped,' she murmured, breathless, responding
almost involuntarily, to the gentleness she had detected
in his voice. And with a gulp which was almost a sob, 'It
was so dark and I knew they were dead . . . and I tried
and tried . . . but I couldn't get out!'

Her voice cracked from the vividness of the nightmare
which had plagued her since childhood and Elliot
prompted quietly, 'Who? Who did you think were dead?'

He was holding her away from him so that he could
look at her, but Fleur couldn't answer him—didn't want
to. She felt a choking sensation and had to swallow hard,
and whether it was from the weakening effects of the
nightmare or not she didn't know, but suddenly she was
sobbing quietly, clinging to the sleeves of his robe with
tears streaming down her cheeks.

'Oh Elliot . . . I haven't done anything wrong,' she got
out between sobs, wanting him to believe her—wanting
him to understand. I haven't . . . I . . . You've got to
believe me . . .'

Her voice tailed off as she felt the flexing of his
muscles—sensed the deep expansion of his chest beneath
the robe. She gazed up at his strong silhouette—hers
submissive—softened by tears and the darkness was
suddenly too intimate—too intense.

His mouth came down to meet hers, tentatively at first,
then with a fierce demand which fired warning signals to
her brain, but she paid no heed to them, her hair falling

like a twist of pale honey as he pushed her back against the pillow.

His hands were unfastening the soft, black shirt. Somewhere in the recesses of her mind a small voice urged her to stop him, but her body was turning traitor against her, welcoming his long, tanned fingers as they slid up over the full, satin mounds of her breasts to caress their hardening peaks, and a deep throaty gasp escaped her.

She had wanted this—for weeks! She had to acknowledge that now. In her wildest fantasies she had imagined being in bed with him, but even those reckless daydreams hadn't prepared her for the extent of his sexual expertise. His hands were cool on her fevered body—unbelievably skilled—moving down over her soft curves with an art he had mastered, evoking a response from her she knew she'd hate herself for afterwards. But this was now and, directed by arousal, her own were moving inside the dark blue robe, revelling in the feel of coarse hair and hard muscle as they caressed the broad chest.

His lips left hers, tracing a line of fire down over her throat to the silken valley of her breasts, and involuntarily she arched her back, her body straining against his, silently begging him to take one aching breast into his mouth.

When he did, the result was explosive. She jerked sharply against him with a strangled cry, relief billowing into a greater, insatiable hunger as sensation fired every nerve into tingling, startling life. Desire coursed through her, producing an acute, throbbing need deep in her loins and tremblingly her fingers twisted in the strong hair at the nape of his neck, catching him to her.

'Oh Fleur...' Her name was an agonised groan and she realised that he was in danger of losing control— battling against his own impassioned desire for her—and then he shifted his position, pulling back the duvet to gaze down upon her inviting nakedness.

'No,' she breathed in protest, suddenly embarrassed—apprehensive—and she reached down for her shirt to draw it across her breasts. But in one swift movement Elliot had caught her hands and was pinning them above her head in one of his own, his dark eyes slumbrous, yet his mouth surprisingly grim.

'Now tell me . . .' His words were harsh and biting, killing the sensual mood with positive brutality. 'If you weren't doing anything wrong, what were you doing with that information?'

Of course, she should have known. The sole purpose of his caresses had been to get her into a position where she'd feel compelled to confess to him. His face was etched with stern lines, and one strong thigh was lodged between her legs so that she couldn't move.

'Who were you getting it for . . . Markham?'

'No!' Panic forced her to deny.

'Yes you were! Tell me the truth!'

'No!' She writhed beneath him and felt his hair-covered thigh brush the soft, inner flesh of hers. But she couldn't admit the truth to him. She didn't know what he would do to her cousin if she did, and guilty or not, she couldn't live with herself if she were answerable for getting him into trouble. 'Let me go,' she choked.

Her body was entirely on view to him, and her trembling breasts still ached from the memory of his touch, their rosy nubs still swollen with arousal. Elliot cast a hard glance over them and Fleur despised herself for her body's betrayal.

'And to think you very nearly had me fooled with those cleverly turned-on tears,' he said contemptuously. 'What were you hoping . . . that I couldn't resist your charms?'

Well he was finding it difficult—even if he could, she thought. And now he was angry with himself because of it. But she hadn't been solely responsible for what had happened.

'I didn't ask you to,' she reminded him, shakily, as he moved away from her, and she could still feel the naked warmth of his skin next to hers.

'No?' She sensed rather than saw the deprecating lift of his eyebrow. 'You didn't exactly do much to try and prevent it, did you?'

Ashamed, Fleur pulled his shirt around her, smarting from the cold disapproval behind his words. No, she hadn't, she realised, and couldn't really understand why. She had never behaved so outrageously before with a man she barely knew—barely liked—and could only put her behaviour down to her vulnerability after that nightmare.

'Neither did you,' she rejoined, sitting up, her tousled hair like a golden frame against her flushed cheeks.

'That's different.'

'Why?' she challenged, incensed by what she considered to be a very male chauvinist remark. 'Because you're a man?'

'No. In my book men and women have an equal responsibility towards each other,' he surprised her by saying, looking down at her as he tied the belt of his robe. 'I'd simply have had some compunction about making love with the person I'd been trying to deceive.' And with that he strode out of the room, leaving her burning with so much shame she couldn't even think of a retort to throw after him.

CHAPTER FOUR

WHEN she got up, the mews appeared surprisingly deserted.

In the shirt and dungarees—her underwear, thankfully dry enough to wear beneath them now—Fleur padded barefoot into the lounge, and then the kitchen, but there was no sign of Elliot. Her ankle didn't hurt half so much this morning, she was glad to discover. She went back along the passageway and noticed that Elliot's bedroom door was half open. Gingerly, Fleur peered through the gap.

A colour-scheme of coffees and creams assured her that this was very much a man's room—from the plain, thick carpet and curtains to the practical design of the duvet on the bed—but it, too, was deserted.

She wondered where he was. Considered, too, how her nightmares had disturbed him during the previous two nights, and she took an almost sadistic pleasure from knowing that he was losing sleep because of keeping her there. But *where* was he? The sun was high, and from the large, digital clock beside Elliot's bed, she was shocked to see that it was after eleven. Her wristwatch had stopped hours before!

Setting it at the right time, she went back into the kitchen and was just making herself a hot drink when the telephone shrilled loudly in the next room.

Fleur paused from pouring hot water into her cup, biting her lower lip as she considered whether or not she should answer it. But a second later she was tearing through into the lounge.

At last! The telephone people had finally reconnected

the line! Now she could contact David!

'Yes. Hello!' She was so excited by this unexpected turn of events—contact with the outside world—she didn't even think to give Elliot's number, and a haughty, female voice was asking, ridiculously,

'Have I got Elliot Steadman?'

Something about the woman's attitude had Fleur biting her tongue to stop herself responding with, Does it sound like it? But she remembered in time that Elliot was a very influential man with a lot of influential business associates and that this superior-sounding female could well be one of them. So in spite of a muzzy head from sleeping too late, she replied in her sweetest voice, 'Yes . . . this is Mr Steadman's private number.'

There was a moment's questioning pause, before the woman exclaimed, 'At last! I've been trying to reach this infernal number for days!' Clearly, she wasn't very pleased that she hadn't been able to. 'Is Elli there?'

Elli? Fleur had to stiffle a giggle. No one looked less like an 'Elli' than the hard-headed king of the Steadman empire. So this was no business associate. The brunette perhaps, who wore pink flowery earrings?

'No, I'm afraid he isn't.' Fleur derived a secret enjoyment from telling her so. 'Can I take a message?'

There was another pause—an impatient drumming of fingernails on the receiver at the other end of the line. Obviously, Miss whoever-she-was wasn't used to leaving messages.

'You're his daily, I suppose?'

The woman's condescending tone sent a bright flush across Fleur's high cheekbones, and it took all her self-control to refrain from erupting with, No, damn you! I'm only his prisoner! But Elliot had made it perfectly clear what action he would take if she tried to escape again, and informing an outsider of her plight could well be deemed as trying to, so she thought better of it. She didn't

want to jeopardise David's future in any way. Keep calm,
she told herself, pressing her lips tightly together and
taking a very deep breath. All you have to do is be nice to
this *pain* and then you can ring him.

'I'm just here on a temporary basis,' she outlined,
cradling the receiver against the soft blush of her cheek.
'Did you have a message?'

'Yes, dear, but do get it right.' The polished tones
incensed, but Fleur held her temper in check. 'Tell Mr
Steadman the party's still on, for tonight. My place.
Eight o'clock.'

That was all. 'Will he know where *my* place is?' Fleur
asked tartly, when the caller failed to offer any clue.

The other woman caught her breath sharply. 'You're
very impertinent for a cleaner. Of course he'll know!' If
the epitome of feminine snobbery sounded unpleasant
before, she sounded thoroughly distasteful now, Fleur
thought. 'It's Gabrielle! Gabrielle Asquith!' And the line
went dead, leaving Fleur staring at the receiver, utterly
piqued.

Well, of all the hoity-toity . . . Quickly, she cut short
her opinion of Gabrielle Asquith. If Elliot wanted to
associate with people like that, then it was no concern of
hers. What did concern her though was getting through
to David. Finding a way out of this awful predicament,
and now! before Elliot came back.

With a sweep of her hand she pushed back her long,
platinum hair and started to dial, her slender fingers
trembling as they picked out the digits for Steadman
International. David had to be in the office. Pray that he
wasn't out with some client! And then she gasped, startled, as a hand with a grip of iron came down hard on her
wrist.

The receiver was being snatched from her hand—
crashed down on its rest—and she swung round, her
amber-flecked eyes wide and alarmed beneath the

burning fury in Elliot's.

'So you'd *still* do it!' His dark features were twisted into harsh, ugly lines, and there was a vein pumping furiously in his temple beneath the deep, Johannesburg tan. 'You little bitch! You wouldn't miss an opportunity to sell that information to Stover's, would you?'

'That isn't true!' She stared up at him, trembling, fixing her gaze on the flat mole on his cheek, too apprehensive to meet his eyes. He was wearing a dark business suit and white shirt, flaunting the image which among his office staff had labelled him, 'the indomitable King Midas'. And to add to that he was wild as well, she thought with a gulp, wincing from the grip in which he still held her. 'I wasn't ringing Stover's. I was trying to get through to someone who might be able to help me . . . someone who would be able to . . . to prove my innocence,' she finished, shakily.

'Then ring him now.'

His slow, casual invitiation surprised her. And as he moved, releasing her, she caught the fresh, tangy scent of his aftershave lotion. He was standing with his fists on his narrow hips, waiting, like a dark, dangerous panther, to spring—waiting for her to make the call.

Fleur looked down at the telephone, licking her lips nervously. Could she? If David hadn't done anything wrong there was nothing to fear, was there? And just because Aunt Aggie used to say that David's ambitions would get the better of him, it didn't mean he'd ever do anything dishonest, did it?

An excrutiating pain of uncertainty brought teardrops tremblingly to her lower lids, and she turned away from the telephone, keeping her face averted so that Elliot wouldn't see them.

'No . . .' he breathed in quiet anger. 'I didn't think you would.'

And she looked at him with moist, sparkling eyes,

wondering why he sounded so sure—wondering how he'd known that it was a man she had been intending to ring. But one thing was certain. Her decision not to had only condemned her still further in his eyes. So much so that they were flickering with a raw, dangerous anger that promised her she was going to pay.

Frightened, she backed away from him, but the table blocked her retreat, and as she made a move to rush past him she came up against the alarming speed of his reflexes. She let out a small sound of protest as he caught her, one arm around her waist, the other tugging her head back by her long, loose hair, forcing her body to meet the hard masculinity of his. She could feel the anger beating in every nerve and sinew in his body, and his breath against the sensitive hollow of her throat came warm and rapidly.

'I ought to take you now ... without mercy,' he breathed with a soft savagery, his mouth coming down on her neck, nipping the delicate flesh. She tensed, fighting this dangerous sexual awareness of him—startled, struggling, as he said, 'I've wanted you in my bed for a long time so why wait any longer? I'll simply take a leaf out of *your* book. Go right ahead and take what I want.'

'No!' Panicking, she tried to stop him as he pulled down the straps of her dungarees. Tried prising his arms away. But he was too strong for her, and his hands were dealing adroitly with the impeding silk shirt—ripping it open.

'No!' As he touched his lips to her shoulder she realised that he wasn't going to be rough at all. His tongue was tracing a sensual line across her skin, making her tremble as she stood rigid in the circle of his arms. Panic was giving way to a primitive excitement, sending a prickly heat along her body, and the shock of her own feelings made her determined to fight harder against

him, so that he laughed without humour, tightening his
hold on her with one strong wall of iron in the small of her
back.

'What's wrong? You wanted me last night.'

His mocking reminder scorched her cheeks with
shame. Dizzy from sensation—from the tantalising tang
of his aftershave lotion—she gasped a feeble, 'No, you're
wrong!' as his dark head swooped to claim the full,
creamy mound of her breast through its thin lace
covering, making her shudder, making her weak. Her
knees were threatening to buckle under her and she
grasped at him for support, felt the muscles beneath the
fine quality jacket tense with desire—but a desire to
punish—to humiliate.

'Elliot . . .' Her small, breathless plea brought his head
up.

Head back, hair tumbling like sun-kissed water, she
stood, body taut, trapped in a well of desire. Eyes closed,
her long, curling lashes lay feathered against the satin
blush of her cheeks, her full lips slightly parted, and a
betraying little pulse was beating frantically in the small
hollow at the base of her throat.

'You're a liar.' Elliot's soft accusation brought her eyes
flickering open. His were dark with smouldering
passion, half-veiled by the thick, black velvet of his
lashes, and his gaze was resting on the thrusting peaks of
her breasts beneath the flimsy lace of her bra. 'You want
me now,' he breathed, raggedly.

She swallowed, shaking her head, too ashamed and
afraid of the sensations in her body to speak.

And suddenly his mouth was descending on hers with
bruising purpose. His hands were on her hips, pressing
them hard against his. She could feel his angry arousal—
the heat emanating from every male pore—and despite
her initial efforts to resist—to push him away—she
began to feel a searing need in her loins as his body

ground against hers, and she was breathing heavily when he finally released her.

'You can deny it all you like ... we both know your body isn't lying, don't we?' he taunted, his hands moving insolently over her soft, feminine curves, so that she hated herself—him!—for this response he could produce in her.

His fingers bit into the tender flesh of her waist, turned across the flat plane of her stomach, moving intimately upwards to caress the creamy smoothness of her breasts again. Heat tingled along her spine, drowning her senses in a warm, sultry tide that was washing over her in waves. She felt desire escalating. And a small moan escaped her as his mouth came down on hers again, but this time with a soft, tender probing which threatened to drive her delirious.

For a few breathless moments she wanted to slide her hands under his jacket—pull open his shirt and feel the damp heat of his skin beneath her fingers. But a sudden tug of respectability was hauling her back to her senses. He wanted to punish her—that was all! So she stood stock-still, withholding the response he had been determined to wring from her, equally determined that he wouldn't.

'A good pretence,' he breathed, lifting his head. There was the twist of a smug smile on his lips, and she knew why. His hand was flat against her heart just under her breast and she knew he could feel the betraying thunder of its beat beneath his fingers. 'Tell me Fleur...' His thumb moved caressingly across the swollen tip of her breast under the wisp of lace, making her shiver with desire. 'How does it feel to want a man you tried to cheat?'

His voice had hardened and stung by his accusation—ashamed of herself for wanting him—Fleur tried to pull away, and realised too late that he wasn't prepared to let her go.

'All right,' she acceded, her breathing coming quickly, her thick, silky hair swishing wildly across her shoulder. 'If you want to humiliate me—make me pay—take what you want!' She was trembling from head to toe now, trembling from the knowledge that whether he tried to take her with brute force or by sheer will-power alone, either way he was going to succeed. But she couldn't let him know that—let him guess how much his dangerous masculinity threatened her. 'Go ahead!' she snapped, her dark eyes sparking anger. 'If you're so determined to make me pay for the sins you're so sure I've committed, then go ahead! Rape me!'

His hold on her relaxed and he took a step back, a dark eyebrow lifting in positive contempt. 'Commit rape? Over an unscrupulous little creature like you?' A muscle tugged at the cruel, sensual mouth. 'You're hardly worth it! No, my tantalising little flower . . .' His hands came to rest on her shoulders—strong and firm—and the determination she could feel oozing out of him made her lick her lips in fear. 'Before you leave here you're going to come to me of your own accord. Willingly! And with your apologies!'

'That's what you think!' She was shaking so much the words seemed to stick in her throat, but he ignored them anyway, turning on his heel and striding out of the room, slamming the door behind him.

So Elliot Steadman had wanted her in his bed for a long time!

Remembering the sensuality with which he had spoken those words earlier, Fleur shuddered from a barrage of confusing emotions. She didn't like him— despised him utterly—for holding her here. Yet she was dangerously attracted to him and knew that if she didn't do something to fight this startling, sexual influence he had over her, his bed was probably where she would inevitably wind up! And he wasn't immune to her either, as he had been claiming all along. Those continual assurances that he was had been only a means of fooling himself, because she knew now that he was burning up with a passion for her which was taking all his self-control to restrain. Last night and this morning had proved that much. Was that his motive then for bringing her here in the first place instead of taking her to the police? she wondered. To get her in bed? After all, he knew he was virtually irresistible to the opposite sex. So was it his intention to get the truth out of her by using that dark, animal magnetism of his and the traitorous responses of her body, thereby taking his revenge and sating his desires at the same time?

She shuddered again from the cold-bloodedness of such an idea as she moved across to the window.

Now I'm becoming paranoid, she thought, staring out at nothing. Elliot had more important issues on his mind at present to be thinking solely about how to effect her surrender. Of course he couldn't take her to the police— not yet anyway. He thought she had vital information to pass on, and even if he did involve the law, how could he be certain that his firm's secrets would still be safe? He couldn't, she found some comfort in acknowledging. That's why he was holding her there. Because he couldn't risk losing the Phoenix deal. Because Frank Steadman had worked himself to death over it. And something told her that Elliot Steadman had loved his father very deeply . . .

A sudden rap on her door interrupted her thoughts, and on her murmured response, it opened.

Elliot looked tired, she thought, as he said, wearily, 'There's a brown soggy mess in a cup out there.' His dark head jerked towards the kitchen. 'Was that an attempt at your breakfast?'

Fleur frowned, then remembered. Of course. She had been pouring water over a tea-bag when the telephone rang. She nodded, giving him the message which had slipped her mind.

'Oh no!' He sounded as if he had forgotten Gabrielle Asquith's party—as if it were too important an occasion for him to miss—and Fleur found herself returning sourly,

'Don't miss it on *my* account!'

'Don't worry . . . I won't.'

His positive declaration surprised her. So what was he proposing to do with her? she wondered. Surely he realised that as soon as he was gone she would be telephoning for help?

Whatever his intention, he was keeping it very much to himself because he said impassively, changing the subject, 'Would you like a more successful attempt at a hot drink?'

Fleur shook her head. She didn't want to take anything from him. So, disinterestedly, he left her, and she went back to gazing out of the window.

She had to get away. Absently watching the antics of a squirrel as it leaped precariously from tree to tree in the park, she wondered what David would be doing. Was he worried about her? Had he asked around the office if anyone had seen her? Been round to the flat to ask her landlady? And the girls whom she worked with—Stacey, June and Trudy—particularly Trudy—surely they must be wondering why she hadn't come in for three days? What excuse had Elliot given them? Or hadn't he bothered? Or worse! Perhaps he'd told them all the truth . . . that she'd broken the firm's trust!

She shivered as she thought about it, not having considered that possibility before. Perhaps everyone knew what she had been doing—albeit innocently—on

Monday. Perhaps he'd told them that she wasn't coming back . . .

She had a sudden, sick feeling in the pit of her stomach and she shook her head violently, trying to rid herself of such dreadful notions. She had to stop thinking like this. Get her mind working on a more positive level. Elliot might be a tough businessman, but he was hardly likely to spread word of one of his staff's supposed crimes to all and sundry in his firm. She had to keep believing that. Otherwise she'd never have the courage to face Steadman International again . . .

Sitting down on the edge of the bed, she cupped her face in her hands, silky, gold strands falling through her fingers as she tried to reason—tried to think. Elliot had said that her ingenuity was highly praised in the office, so where was that ingenuity now? Why couldn't she think of a way to get herself out of here? Get to David? Clear up this whole terrible mess once and for all?

Staring down through her fingers at the urgent rise of her young breasts, at her long, slender legs in the dungarees, the idea suddenly came to her. She was a woman, wasn't she? With a woman's functioning? With totally different needs from Elliot? So why not make those needs work for her?

Quickly she jumped up, her heart thumping hard. She wasn't sure, but it might just work.

He was sitting, dark head bent over some paperwork on the table, but looked up as she padded barefoot into the room.

'You've got to let me out,' she said in a small voice.

'No.' Elliot's answer was final and, as if to give it more strength, he turned back to his work.

'You have to.' She moved closer to him—the rich warmth of the carpet an almost tangible sensuality beneath her feet—and she was slightly breathless from the thought of challenging him, but this was her only hope. 'The course of Nature doesn't stop even for you, Elliot Steadman,' she asserted in defiance, and with an unaccountable little tremor, 'I need a chemist.'

He'd detected that tremor, she could tell. And from the way he was looking at her—grey eyes narrowing, assessing, as they raked over her body—she had the awful feeling that he knew she wasn't telling him the truth. But, of course, he couldn't be certain, even when guilt brought a tinge of colour to her cheeks. And she knew he wouldn't go out himself and leave her there alone now that the telephone was working, so really he had no choice.

His sharp, indrawn breath was proof of it. 'All right,' he accepted, reluctantly, folding away his papers and pocketing his pen. 'Come along.'

It was good to be out. Suspecting that it would be cold, Fleur had changed into her woollen dress and was glad that she had, although the bright freshness of the cool day was revitalising—enlightening—to her low spirits.

Her bluff had worked well in getting her out of the mews. She glanced across at Elliot as he drove her towards the shops, and wondered, as her eyes met that strong, thrusting profile, just what he would do to her if he found out that she had been lying to him. She swallowed uneasily, turning to stare out of the windscreen. There was only one way he could find out, wasn't there? she tried reassuring herself, as the car stopped at a pedestrian crossing to allow several teenage schoolchildren to cross. And that was only if she succumbed to that dark and dangerous sensuality. And she certainly wasn't going to do that! Nevertheless, a sharp twinge of desire made itself felt in her loins as she recalled the thrilling effects of his touch, and rebelliously she drove the sensation away by giving full concentration to the more important matter ahead.

She had to ring David. Escape was foolish even to
think about because Elliot had promised to ruin her
career prospects and David's if she tried again, and she
was taking his threat seriously. But if she could persuade
Elliot to take her to one of the large stores, well . . . they
had telephones, didn't they? Perhaps she could get to one
under the pretext of going to the cloakroom. After all, she
did need tights . . .

'No,' he stated firmly, when she suggested one,
thrusting the car into gear and completely ignoring her
protests that she couldn't buy her favourite brand of
hosiery anywhere else. 'You asked for a chemist,' he
reminded her coolly, as the Jaguar growled menacingly
into motion again. 'And a chemist is all you're going to
get.'

He kept his word, not allowing her out of his sight as
she moved through the crowded shop, made her
purchases, including some tights and shampoo, and then
followed him dispiritedly back to the car.

She could have cried. Especially when Elliot eased
himself into the driving seat again and started the
engine, and she knew for certain that all her efforts had
been for nothing.

He was no fool. Not that she had ever suspected him of
being one. But she knew now that she couldn't get away
from him, not even for a moment. Not until, as he'd
promised her so resolutely days ago, the Phoenix deal
was finalised.

She didn't know whether he sensed some of her
frustration, but as they motored away from the busy
shopping precinct, he swung a glance towards her and in
a surprisingly soft tone, asked, 'Are you hungry?'

She nodded, her blonde hair catching the light with the
barest movement. She wasn't though. She didn't feel at
all hungry—only numb, sick inside. And she couldn't
understand why Elliot wasn't angry with her—livid. He

must surely have guessed what was behind this excursion into town, even if he had accepted her feeble excuse back at the mews. He must have known that once out, she'd be racking her brains to try and find some way of getting to a phone. Why else would he have refused to take her to one of the larger stores? And as far as he was concerned, she needed a telephone to pass vital information on to a rival company. So why wasn't he angry with her? Wild?

She stared out of the window on her side of the car, toying anxiously with a fraying watchstrap. There was only one answer to that. He knew she couldn't outwit him, even if she'd only just realised it herself. She was completely under his control, so any anger on his part would have been a pointless emotion. All she sensed in him now was that familiar contempt, mingling with a humiliating shred of pity. The sort one felt for a cornered animal . . .

He took her to a small inn-restaurant—a half-timbered building with exposed beams, red carpets and curtains to match the wall-lamps, and a tiny dining-room through the far end of the bar. As yet, only a couple of tables were occupied, Fleur noticed, glancing round. A young couple gazed dreamily at each other at the table next to their own, while across the room a middle-aged couple were arguing audibly with their teenage children over the subject of modern music.

The place was warm—cosy and snug—but her bare legs were freezing, and catching sight of a cloakroom sign, Fleur made to get up.

'Where are you going?' A heavy hand was on her wrist, and Elliot's grey eyes were flashing a warning above the menu he had been studying.

'To put on some tights, if you don't mind!' Fleur shot back, sourly, brown eyes dancing in anger. 'Or are you going to come down there with me as well?'

He released her. 'What do you want to eat?'

He sounded cool, unperturbed, and she shrugged, mouth twisting indifferently. 'You order for me,' she said.

Sheathing her legs in sheer nylon, Fleur brushed her hair, and deciding that there was too little colour in the soft oval face, added a touch of blusher to the high cheekbones.

She looked strained, she thought, studying her reflection. There was an anxious crease between her eyes, and dark shadows beneath them from losing sleep. Even her mouth seemed to have lost its gentle curvature, but then, she accepted, painfully, she had very little to smile about at present. The sight of her woebegone self did nothing to lift her spirits and she turned away from the mirror, taking the few steps back to the dining-room when something stopped her dead in her tracks. She couldn't believe it! On the lobby wall, between the two respective cloakrooms, was a pay-phone!

For a split second she hesitated—heart hammering wildly. And the next moment she was ramming in coins. Her hands were shaking so much she could hardly hold her money, but she was through! and a familiarly-friendly voice was saying at the other end of the line, 'Fleur! What on earth's happened to you? There's been a rumour going round the office that you sprained your ankle, but nobody seems to know for sure!' Trudy Marshall's exuberant personality would have been appreciated at any other time, but at that moment all Fleur wanted was to be connected with David's office.

'Look ... I can't explain now,' she started in a rush, shooting a furtive glance towards the restaurant door—all that afforded protection from Elliot and a chance to speak to her cousin—but Steadman's telephonist, she realised with a sinking heart, was in a chatty mood.

'It's been busy here this morning even without our

lord and master breathing down our necks! I thought we might have had an easier time of it while he's been moving house, but I'd swear he governs this office by remote control! Wowee! What a man!' Fleur heard the whistle of appreciation Trudy expressed, and she tapped her foot impatiently.

'Trudy . . .' She tried again, but there was no stopping the other girl and Fleur remembered with sickening dismay that Elliot Steadman was Trudy's favourite subject.

'I just wish he'd hurry up and come back,' she went on, quite unaware of Fleur's increasing tension. 'The place is drab without that delectable animal around. And to add to everything else the drinks machine's broken down,' she wailed, 'and I'd give a pound for a cup of coffee! I don't know what . . .'

'Look Trudy . . .' Fleur gritted her teeth, the blood pounding at her temples as she banged a clenched fist against the wall. 'I'm in danger of being cut off and I haven't got another coin,' she put in quickly, hating having to lie. But she fully expected Elliot to come tearing down the stairs looking for her at any minute, and this was one opportunity of reaching her cousin that she was not going to miss. 'I'll talk to you later, but can you put me through to David.'

'Connecting you!' The redhead's bright, sing-song words were like music to her ears. But in seconds Trudy was back. 'Sorry, Fleur . . . what a clown I am! He hasn't been in since Monday. He's obviously working away this week.'

'Oh dear . . .' She couldn't help the small, hopeless groan which escaped her.

'Hey, Fleur . . . are you all right?' Trudy queried, sensing something was wrong.

'Yes, yes,' Fleur answered swiftly, anxious to get off the line. 'I'll talk to you later, all right?'

She didn't wait for Trudy's reply. Already she was searching for another coin, and her heart was in her mouth as she heard David's home number ringing. He couldn't be working away. He would have told her on Monday if he'd been expecting to be.

When he answered she could have sobbed there and then. And when he said, 'Fleur . . . thank God!' she did.

CHAPTER FIVE

'WHERE are you, Fleur . . . where are you?'

Through an overwhelming release of emotion she heard her cousin's voice, urgent—concerned—and she took a deep breath, sniffing back tears.

'I'm in the lobby of some little pub. Oh David! I've been trying to ring you all week . . .'

'What are you doing . . .' His question tailed off, puzzlement in his tone. 'Where have you been? Why couldn't you ring me? I've been waiting for your call.'

Her gaze shot towards the door through which she expected Elliot to burst at any moment, and she said quickly, 'Oh David! I'm in terrible trouble! It's all over that information you asked me to find for you on Monday . . . Elliot came in and caught me! He said no one knew that password except him and some of the Board Members and I couldn't understand . . . I didn't . . . !' She was gabbling, her voice rising almost hysterically. 'David . . . what did he mean?',

'What are you doing in a pub?' he queried, not answering her.

'He thinks I'm trying to sell something or other to Stover's so he's holding me prisoner until the Phoenix deal goes through. He . . .'

'He's what!' The vehemence behind his shocked response made Fleur recoil somewhat, but she derived a sudden comfort from it nevertheless. David wouldn't allow Elliot to hold her like this any longer. 'Is he with you now?'

'Yes . . .' She raised an anxious face towards the door again. 'Well no . . . he's in the din . . .'

'You didn't tell him anything about me?' His urgent interruption startled her—then, as she grasped it—seemed to knock her off-balance.

'No . . . I didn't know what to do. I . . .' She broke off, and through her comfort felt a knot tightening in the pit of her stomach. 'Elliot thinks I stole that password. That I . . . that you . . . David, where did you get it?' Her heart was beating so fast with apprehension that she felt sick. 'You didn't . . .'

'For heaven's sake, calm down!' Through a daze of uncertainty she heard her cousin's sharp recommendation. 'Of course I didn't steal it!' There was a deep pause, a moment when relief coursed through Fleur's veins, relief so strong she thought her legs were going to give way. With a deep sigh she closed her eyes, tears moistening the feathery lashes—dark against the pallor of her skin—and like that she heard David say, 'If I'm guilty of stealing, then every newspaperman and T.V. reporter should be questioned as to how they get their information. It all boils down to the same thing, love. Take what's up for grabs and sell it to anyone who'll pay.'

Fleur opened her eyes and stared at the mouthpiece, relief giving way to a cold, nauseating revulsion. It couldn't be true! She put a hand on the wall to steady herself, feeling remarkably in danger of collapsing. Was this the cousin she had grown up with—loved like a brother? The cousin she'd been suffering all week to protect? Taking Elliot's hard accusatiors and contempt because she'd believed David was as innocent as she was? For the first time she realised that she didn't really know her cousin at all.

Her voice was a thin whisper as she said, 'Then you did . . .' And when he didn't answer, 'And you tried to involve me?' Anger put back the strength in her voice. 'Why? Why? David?'

'I'm sorry, Fleur' His tone contradicted that statement.

'I thought it would be safest, with you using the computer all the time. If I'd been seen using it . . .' There was a pause as if he had shrugged. 'When I heard you'd been caught . . .'

'You knew!' She gripped the receiver tightly, knuckles showing white, dark eyes flashing wildly as she demanded, 'How? How could you have known?'

All sorts of raging thoughts were tearing at her—like had Elliot told people—perhaps senior personnel—what he'd found her doing? And she still felt herself breaking out into a sweat even when David explained, 'It was something Tom Bowman said. You know . . . the night-watchman? When you didn't come in Tuesday morning I shot round to your flat. I thought you were ill. When you weren't there I didn't go back to the office until everyone had gone. I thought perhaps one of the night staff might have been able to tell me something.'

Fleur listened, hardly taking it in, the fingers of her free hand twisting painfully in her hair.

'Bowman told me he'd seen you leaving with Elliot on Monday night . . . and I guessed you'd been caught trying to get that data.'

'You knew all along . . . and you didn't do anything about it? Didn't you wonder what had happened to me?' She couldn't believe it—couldn't comprehend that he could abandon her like that. 'You could have gone to the police.'

'And got myself slung in jail? Be realistic, Fleur. What could I do? All I could do was wait for you to ring me. You know I wouldn't have landed you in this mess on purpose, don't you?'

She couldn't answer, too stunned to say anything, hurting too much inside even to feel. All her mind could register was that he was guilty. That all her fears and her frightening suspicions over the past few days were totally founded. And David didn't sound the least bit sorry.

'Fleur?'

She rested her head against the booth, her blonde hair falling forward. 'Yes . . . yes I'm still here.' Was that *her* voice? So agonised? So weary?

'I didn't dream for one moment that anyone would come in and find you. I'm sorry.' His further attempt at an apology sounded less sincere than the last. 'Elliot was supposed to be away . . .'

Elliot! A surge of adrenalin pumped through her, and she shot another glance towards the door. She'd been ages! If she didn't hurry up and go back to the dining-room, she had no doubt at all that he would come looking for her.

'David, you've got to help me!' Gripping the receiver with both hands, she gasped, startled when the door opened, her heart in her mouth.

The dark-haired girl who had been sitting at the next table gave her a half-smile before passing into the cloakroom, and Fleur began to breathe again.

'David . . . you've got to tell Elliot what you've done!' she urged in a lower tone. 'Make a clean breast of things before he finds out for himself. I'm sure he won't . . .'

'You're joking?' was the prompt, satirical reply. 'I'm getting out while I can. Did you get any of that information?'

Fleur hesitated, not sure what he meant. Then realised that he was referring to Phoenix.

'Yes,' she started, puzzled, 'but . . .'

'Then let me have it.'

'No!' Horror twisted her mouth from the abhorrence of what he still intended to do. 'I'm not doing anything against the firm . . . and I'm not going to let you, either,' she stressed, a sob in her voice. 'You've got to . . . David!'

Rapid pips had her rummaging frantically through her purse for more coins, but it was already too late. The line had gone dead. And there was no point in ringing him back. Somehow she knew that if it meant owning up to what he had done, David wasn't going to help her, and if she stayed away from the restaurant any longer, she knew she would have Elliot to deal with.

A cold emptiness settled inside her. David had used her, and now, to save his own skin, he was leaving her to get out of this predicament all by herself. She was too hurt even to cry any more. Quickly she dusted her cheeks with face powder to hide the traces of her tears, and showering herself with *Femme* cologne so that Elliot would think she'd been all this time freshening up, she made her way back to the dining-room.

She was scarcely through the door when she saw him striding purposefully towards her, his face grim, although the taut lines relaxed a little when he saw her and Fleur caught her breath. She'd only just made it by the skin of her teeth!

'You took your time,' he muttered, following her back to their table.

She flashed him a bitter-sweet smile as he pulled out her chair—his manners superlative even though his eyes condemned.

'Were you frightened I'd run away?' she queried, brittly. And flinched as he bent low, hands on the back of her chair, his lips so close to her hair that she could feel his breath on her cheek, smell the tangy lemon of his aftershave lotion.

'I trusted you weren't that stupid.' Though he spoke softly, there was a definite undercurrent of anger behind his words. 'I don't make idle threats, Fleur . . . remember that. I can break you, and that charming cousin of yours without any compunction whatsoever . . . so if you want some sort of future in the business world you'd better not do anything foolish . . . for his sake as well as your own.' He straightened so that she was suddenly aware again of how powerfully built he was—how potentially dangerous. 'After all . . . you care rather a great deal for your cousin don't you?' he hissed, his eyes hardening on hers, and she had to struggle to hold back a fresh surge of tears. Yes, she'd cared very much, once, but that had been when he was still a gangling teenager, and she'd been just a child . . .

'Of course I do . . . we were brought up together,' she threw back somewhat shakily. 'He was like a brother to me.'

'Was?' From the seat across the table, Elliot studied her hard. 'What about now?'

There was accusation in his harsh demand and Fleur lowered her gaze, refusing to answer him. Clearly, he'd already drawn his own conclusions about now.

He didn't press the subject since a plump, red-faced woman waddled to their table with two steaming bowls of vegetable soup.

'Lovely day again for the time of year,' she commented with a smile which embraced them both, but her twinkling blue eyes were resting appreciatively on Elliot.

'Perfect.' He gave the woman such an arresting smile before she moved away, that Fleur recognised an absurd pang of envy. He had never smiled at *her* like that. And probably never will after what he thinks I've done, she ruminated, thoughts of the telephone conversation she had had with David chilling her to the bone.

How could she tell Elliot the truth now? she wondered, worriedly, spooning her soup. He'd have the police round to David's flat before she could draw breath. But what about when the Phoenix deal was settled . . . when Elliot fired her as he was obviously going to? He'd realise that David was involved at once if her cousin left the company without a word, but if she told Elliot the truth then, would be believe her? Absently, she broke her bread roll, anxiety and some other indefinable emotion gnawing at her as she admitted to herself that she didn't think he would. He'd probably think she was involved, too, and simply trying to save her own skin—her own career—and there was no way that she could prove otherwise unless David owned up . . .

'You're very subdued today. Conscience troubling you?' Elliot had finished his soup and was examining her with cold, grey eyes, and Fleur couldn't help the mutinous look which instantly sprang to her own.

'I'd have thought you'd have realised by now that I don't have one,' she returned caustically, toying with her soup. It was thick and delicious—made on the premises—and the bread was warm, too, but she hardly tasted it. In fact, she put down her spoon before she had finished, and noticed the questioning lift of Elliot's dark eyebrow.

'Not hungry?'

She shook her blonde head, sipping her wine for something to do as she looked away from his deprecating gaze.

The restaurant was filling up. Most of the tables were occupied now. The family who had been arguing had gone—even their table was re-occupied, and there was a gentle hub-hub of conversation filtering around them with some soft, background music—an enveloping air of warmth, good humour and contentment which she couldn't share.

'You look tired.' Her mind was brought back to her own table with a jolt. Elliot was leaning towards her, his arms resting on the table, and this time she couldn't look away from that penetrating gaze, much as she wanted to. It seemed to lock with hers, and hold her there. 'Was it really worth it, Fleur?' There was something other than contempt in his voice. Sympathy? No surely not? she thought, dismissively. She was imagining it, just as she had imagined the transient softening of those grey eyes.

But his chest was broad and strong beneath the dark jacket and for a moment she had an overwhelming urge to bury her head against it and sob out the whole, miserable truth. Except that he probably wouldn't believe her . . .

The plump woman had returned and Fleur was grateful. It meant that Elliot's attention was diverted away from her for a while. But when they were alone again, she said, accusingly, 'And if I look tired, broken sleep and nightmares don't do very much for one's appearance.'

The dark eyebrows lifted slightly. 'Are you blaming *me* for that?'

Fleur raised her head on her slender neck, a soft moue to her lips. 'The nightmares wouldn't have started again if you . . .'

'You've had them before?' Interest was flickering in the grey eyes, and his hand came up to support his chin, while he studied her thoughtfully. 'When?'

She didn't like his cold, calculated scrutiny and she glanced away, absently surveying a tall, moustached man who was serving at another table. 'I hardly think it's important,' she rejoined icily.

'On the contrary.' Elliot's deep response made her look back, surprised. 'I think it is.',

'Why?' A flush was spreading across her cheeks and her eyes were suddenly flashing hurt anger within the soft oval of her face. 'So you can work out what makes the criminal, female mind tick?'

His mouth simply quirked in response, and she realised why. The second course had arrived—a Chicken Chasseur which he had ordered for them both—and the woman served them making light, amiable conversation from which Fleur learned that the man with the moustache was her husband, and the proprietor.

'We believe in giving our customers the personal

touch,' she admitted, beaming at them both, and Fleur
smiled back, thinking how homely the woman was, how
much like her Aunt Aggie, and after the proprietress had
gone, couldn't help murmuring, 'She's nice.'

'That's debatable.' Fleur looked questioningly at
Elliot—saw the wry twist to his lips, as he said
abrasively, 'She thinks you're my wife.'

She coloured instantly, and wasn't sure why. The
woman must have been talking to Elliot while she herself
was in the cloakroom, she guessed—must have mistaken-
ly assumed them to be husband and wife—but one thing
was certain. Elliot found the suggestion most distasteful.

'How dreadful for you,' she replied, pungently, biting
her lower lip, hurt, more than she cared to admit that
such a thought should totally repel him. True, she didn't
relish the thought of being tied to him either for life, but
he was a man of principle—despite everything, she was
certain of that—and that such a man should hold such a
low opinion of her own ethics stung.

'Tell me about your nightmares.' He was about to pour
her some more wine but she stopped him in time, placing
her hand over her glass.

'Ah yes,' he remembered, a derisive curl to his lips.
'Little Miss Virtue never has more than one, does she?'

She flinched almost perceptibly from his cold, cutting
sarcasm, saying nothing. She didn't feel like talking to
him.

'How long have you been having these ... bad
dreams?' Elliot's question drifted lazily across the table
as she tried in vain to do justice to the beautifully-
prepared food. 'When did they first start?'

He was determined to pursue the subject—that was
obvious—and exasperated, Fleur put down her knife and
fork, deciding to let him have it with both barrels.

'If you really want to know ... they're something I
grew up with!' she fired at him, amber-flecks dancing

furiously in the wide, brown eyes. 'And if you're so
determined to play the Freudian shrink,' she continued,
heatedly, 'then you can have it straight! I was involved in
a car crash when I was seven years old! My mother and
father were in the front and they were both killed
outright. I wasn't hurt but I was trapped in the back for
an hour before anybody came and found us because the
car only had two doors and I couldn't get out!' She said it
virtually in one breath, shuddering involuntarily, the
horror of that night still so vivid in her mind it was
bringing her out into a cold sweat. Her palms were sticky
from just talking about it. 'And before you ridicule my
aversion to alcohol, *Dr Freud*,' she added, venomously, 'I
think you should know that the driver responsible for
killing my parents was drunk!'

She closed up then, like a clam, and picking up her
fork began pushing a piece of chicken aggressively round
her plate.

It was a few moments before Elliot said quietly, 'I'm
sorry,' and glancing up she had to admit that he really
looked as if he were. The restaurant's red lights were
emphasising the red in his hair, but his eyes were
darkened by concern, and a little compunction, too, she
suspected. He'd looked like that before, she thought,
probing her memory, and recalled that it was when she'd
told him her aunt had died, just after he'd taken over as
Steadman's Chairman. The hard mask had fallen away
for a few moments and she'd found him surprisingly
understanding, expressing his condolences with all the
empathy of his own bereavement. She remembered she'd
warmed to him then—briefly.

Shrugging, she said, 'It was a long time ago,' and
picking up her fork again, tried to eat something else.
Elliot was well on the way to emptying his plate.

'Who brought you up?' he was asking. 'Relatives?'
Fleur nodded. 'Well ... just my aunt—David's

mother—because my uncle was killed in a tin-mining accident a year later.'

She couldn't stop her voice from cracking over her cousin's name and she thought Elliot's mouth hardened.

'And you're still affected by that awful experience?' He was referring to the nightmares again, and she responded with, 'The doctor said I'd probably grow out of them, and I did for a time . . . only they came back again during my A levels and . . .'

'And?' he prompted when she didn't finish.

Well, why shouldn't she tell him? He thought the worst of her anyway.

'When I first came to London . . . I shared a flat with someone . . .' She looked down at her plate, feeling a flush stealing across her cheeks.

'I see.' There was a wealth of meaning behind those two words and she looked up to meet Elliot's cool mockery. 'Not so virtuous after all,' he assessed, softly.

Over the murmur of conversation and gentle music his words goaded so that she threw back in defence, 'I thought I loved him.'

He smirked. 'But you found out you didn't?'

'Something like that.' She resumed picking at her lunch, the heavy silk of her hair falling in a deep, gold wave against her shoulder. Impartially, she wondered what had happened to the boy who had followed her here from Cornwall. Moved into her home and her bed and after a few brief weeks, moved out again. The last she had heard of him he had gone back to the West Country and married someone else. 'He couldn't stand the nightmares anyway, so it wouldn't have worked out,' she murmured, casually.

The young couple at the next table got up to leave and Fleur noticed that they were holding hands. They were obviously very much in love, she thought, and knew a moment's cold isolation. She had never been that close to anyone for any length of time . . .

'Did you feel trapped?'

Elliot's question startled her. Now why had he asked that? Because she had, she realised, in retrospect. Yet she'd never connected that feeling with the dreams she'd been having at the time.

'Yes, I did,' she answered, guilelessly, rather unsettled by the way Elliot had put two and two together so easily. 'At eighteen, neither of us were ready for the responsibilities of a commitment.'

'I should damn well think not.'

It was clear he disapproved of such young matches, and Fleur watched him as he finished his meal, guessing that not at any time in his life would he have made such an impetuous decision as she had done. He was shrewd, capable and self-reliant, knowing exactly where he was going in life—making the right decisions and seeing them through. And he was undeniably attractive, too, she thought, her gaze running discreetly over the rugged planes of his face. That mole on his left cheek was alluring in itself, even without the cruel sensuality of that hard mouth, and the arresting command of that strong jaw. And of their own accord her eyes followed the movement of his hands as he applied the napkin to his mouth. They were long and tanned against the whiteness of his shirt-cuff, perfectly tapered, and those dark, silky hairs running down the back of them spoke volumes of his virility. There was no doubt about it, thought Fleur, with a sharp kick of desire in her loins. He would probably be incredible in bed. And was shocked to realise that she was fighting an intense, burning hunger to find out.

'Have you finished?'

She blushed as he spoke to her, having the uncomfortable feeling that he could read her thoughts, but he was frowning down at her plate—at the barely touched chicken—and she nodded.

'Perhaps I should have wrung that apology out of you first.' She bit her lip, colouring scarlet. Did he still intend to?

His eyes were glacial as they bored into hers, and his mouth was rigid with determination. Yes, he did, she thought, her heart thumping hard against her rib-cage. Only he'd said she would come to him willingly, but she wouldn't. She wouldn't! And why should she tell him *anything* when he refused to let her go?

'You can take that rebellious look off your face right now,' he recommended with a quiet harshness, 'because you . . .'

The shrill bleeping sound cut him short and instantly he flicked off the switch on the small device he was wearing on his waistband—a device which kept him in continual contact with his firm—and was getting swiftly to his feet.

'Get your coat. We're leaving.'

The sudden urgency after the relatively leisurely meal came as rather a shock to Fleur.

'Where are we going?' she asked, puzzled.

'Just get your coat . . . I'll settle the bill.'

Obviously Elliot was in an uncommunicative mood, and it wasn't until they were on the road that Fleur tried again with, 'Well at least tell me where we're going.'

'I've some business to attend to.'

That was all he was offering, and whatever his business was, it was important Fleur decided, because she had never seen anyone drive so fast in her life. This was real aggression, she realised, watching him thrust the car into gear and overtake everything in sight, taking the bends in a way which, had anyone else been driving, she would have considered reckless, yet which, with Elliot, only seemed to emphasise his capability and control. The way he manoeuvred the Jaguar swiftly and easily

through the hectic, London traffic was a work of art, and
she recognised a sudden surge of admiration for him.
That was until he pulled into his company's covered car
park, and then all other feelings were doused by a raging
dread that the moment of reckoning had come.

Fear gnawed at her stomach as he led her across the
tarmac to his own private lift, and as they ascended to the
executive suite, her throat constricted painfully.

So this is it, she thought, plunging her hands into the
pockets of her trench coat and clenching them tightly—
holding herself rigid so that the man beside her wouldn't
notice how much she was trembling.

Had that been the purpose of the meal? she wondered,
anguishedly. To try and psychoanalyse her—find out
how her mind worked before he hauled her up before the
other Board members? She didn't think she could
stand that!

She shot him a furtive glance. He looked hard and dark
and forbidding. Yet difficult though it was, she knew she
would rather tell him the truth while they were alone,
than have him drag it out of her in front of the entire
Board, because in the formality of his Boardroom, she
knew he would be as merciless as a prosecuting barrister
in his own private court.

Her throat felt dry and she swallowed, trying to find
the right words. 'Elliot . . . I've got to tell you . . .'

'Not now!' he snapped, impatiently cutting her short
as the lift whined to a halt, and a moment later he was
ushering her into his office.

'Wait here,' he commanded, and almost as an
afterthought, unplugged the external telephone and
tossed it into a drawer of the filing cabinet, securing it
with a key. 'Just so you won't be tempted,' he advised in
cold humour before leaving her.

Alone, behind the closed door, Fleur paced up and
down the thickly carpeted floor, wondering what was

going to happen next. He hadn't locked her in. He'd
known it wasn't necessary. He had made her only too
aware already of what he would do if she tried to escape,
and she wasn't foolish enough to jeopardise her own
future even if David hadn't cared about his.

She looked around the office. It was plush. She hadn't
seen it since Frank Steadman had died and vaguely her
mind registered that Elliot had removed some of the
original paintings and added others more suiting to his
taste, as well as a long, low couch and another bookcase.

She sat down on the couch. Thought better of it and
stood up again, a knot tightening excruciatingly in her
stomach. Looking at her gold wristwatch she noticed that
only ten minutes had gone by since Elliot had left her.
And when she looked again it was fifteen.

She was shivering—yet hot and clammy—and tossing
her trench coat over the back of a chair, she went over to
stand by the window. Diminutive traffic was weaving its
way through the busy square, twelve floors below, and
Fleur stared down at it, twisting a blonde strand
agitatedly around her finger.

Why didn't he hurry up ... get it over with? she
wondered anxiously, looking at her watch again. Why
was it taking him twenty-five minutes to tell them what
she had done? Or what he thought she had done, she
corrected, grimacing. The knot in her stomach became
nauseating as the minutes ticked by, and still Elliot didn't
come. She felt sick. Went to his private shower-room and
found that she couldn't be. And then for something to do
she applied fresh powder and lipstick, coming back into
the office just as the door was opening.

'Fleur!' Andrew Moreton looked nothing less than
embarrassed. He laughed awkwardly. 'Fleur . . .' He said
again, stroking a rather brightly patterned tie. 'I didn't
expect to find you here . . .'

That much was obvious. His face was unusually

flushed beneath his wiry, brown hair and there were
traces of cigarette ash on his jacket. And that was a bad
sign, Fleur realised, because Andrew only smoked these
days when things were going wrong. So Elliot must have
just told him about me, she thought, with a pain in her
stomach which made her want to double up, and from
the way the older man was edging towards the door, he
couldn't get away fast enough.

'Waiting for Elliot?' he asked, perfunctorily, and when
she nodded, muttered, 'Oh well . . . I don't expect he'll be
long,' before making a hasty exit out of the office.

Desolation washed over her. She had always liked
Andrew Moreton. And now, because of her stupidity—
her childish hope and trust in David, believing he'd
never do anything wrong—her silence had probably
convicted her—killed the former respect Andrew had
had for her, along with that of the rest of the Board, but
above all, any Elliot might have had for her. And,
inexplicably, that thought hurt most.

She swung round as he came in—found herself riveted
to the spot by the intensity of his gaze. Darkly
dominating, in striking contrast to his second-in-
command, Elliot's immaculate appearance seemed to
emphasise the hard authority in him—the leadership—
while the penetrating grey eyes seemed to be cutting into
her like cold slate. Beneath the white, silk shirt his chest
was rising heavily, and with a shudder Fleur guessed that
whatever he had been saying in that Boardroom,
someone had felt the blast of his anger.

And now it's my turn, she thought, as he said, heavily,
'Are you ready?'

'Yes.' It came out on a trembling breath.

With impeccable courtesy he held the door open for
her and as she moved past him, her hand accidentally
brushed his so that she was tingling as he led her back
along the corridor—tingling and apprehensive and

miserable.

He was going to fire her. And during those forty lonely minutes she had spent in his office, she'd decided that she was going to let him without any argument. Whatever he thought of her—the Board thought of her— she couldn't clear her own name without convicting David, and though they would find out the truth soon enough, even though David had left her to save his own skin, she still couldn't do anything which might lead to his being sent to prison. Also, she didn't think she could work for Steadman's after this—even if she were proved innocent—knowing what her cousin had tried to do against them. Even if he owned up to his crime, she would never be able to bear the whispers behind her back—the sympathy from everyone in the office when they found out why David had left. But worst of all, after the way her body had responded to Elliot's—knowing how he could make her feel now simply by walking into the same room—she didn't think she would ever be able to work under him again, knowing that he knew . . .

'Where are we going?'

She had been so absorbed in her misery she hadn't realised he had been leading her back to the lift, and she looked at him, puzzled.

'My dear girl, that seems to be becoming your stock phrase,' he drawled with cool mockery, pressing the button for the car park.

She could see now that he was carrying her coat over his arm and a frown knit her finely arched brows. 'I thought . . .'

'You thought what?' He stared at her hard, his dark features inexorable, yet oozing such a potent sexuality that she felt like a moth in danger of being drawn too close to a flame.

'I thought you were going to have me up before the Board . . .' Brown eyes met grey and held them. 'That you'd brought me here this afternoon to fire me.'

'Did you?' In the confines of the lift he seemed unnervingly big, and Fleur moistened her lips as he moved closer to her. His arm came to rest on the wall of the lift, just above her shoulder, and he was so near that she pressed herself hard against the wall, afraid of accidentally touching him again. 'I told you,' he murmured, his breath stirring a few strands of the soft, blonde hair. 'You're going to give your explanations and apologies to me first ... however long it takes. And perhaps now might be a good time to start!'

A small protest escaped her when he hit a button so hard on the switch panel that the lift juddered to a halt.

'Perhaps you'd care to tell me now that you haven't been alone in this ... deception. That David's as involved as you are?'

She looked at him, brown eyes startled, realising he was so near the truth that she could only gulp, 'What makes you say that?'

'He is, isn't he?'

She didn't know what to say. She wondered how he had come to suspect her cousin—whether something had been said in the office this afternoon or whether Elliot had seen through David all along when she'd been too blind to—but the thought of his guilt brought a painful lump to her throat and she couldn't speak.

Elliot looked grim. 'Are you going to admit of your own free will that you've been covering up for him as well, or am I going to have to coax it out of you with more unorthodox means?'

'No!' She tried to move away. Found she couldn't when his other arm came up to prevent it—totally imprisoning her against the wall—but he hadn't actually touched her and anger welled up inside her, dissipating fear.

'I keep telling you! I'm not guilty of anything! And

certainly not of a cover up!' she expostulated, though there were hot tears burning her eyes from the torturing knowledge that if she didn't tell him the truth now, she would be doing exactly that of which he was accusing her. 'If you're so sure David's guilty, then why don't you ask him?' she suggested, vehemently, 'instead of bullying . . .'

She broke off as the light above them suddenly went out and then flickered on again, and without thinking she grasped at his sleeve.

She had never liked lifts. Use them though she did, it was always with a raging claustrophobia—a dread that if the mechanics failed she could be in a situation where she was utterly trapped—and already she could feel the perspiration breaking out all over her body.

But she felt the consolation of a strong hand against her shoulder. Heard Elliot's, 'It's all right. We haven't broken down.' And she wondered whether that gentle concern in his voice really had been there, or if she had imagined it, but she put it to the back of her mind because the doors were opening and they were in the car park again.

CHAPTER SIX

'YOU'RE joking!' she had said. 'I'm not going to any party with you!'

But putting the finishing touches to her make-up, Fleur found herself acknowledging with a small shudder just how determined Elliot could be.

'It's business as well as pleasure so unfortunately I have to attend,' she remembered him saying that afternoon. 'And since I've no intention of trusting you alone in the mews with a fully operating telephone, I'm just going to have to take you with me ... painful though that night prove to be ... for both of us.' His words had dropped on to her like icicles as he pulled up outside her flat, insisting that she obtain a change of clothes.

And when she had countered, brittly, 'And if I refuse to come?' he had simply threatened to carry her down to the car and deliver her to the Asquiths exactly as she was—in her grubby, woollen dress—so that pride, and the jolting memory of his lady-friend's superior attitude over the telephone, had forced her to comply.

Well, why shouldn't she go to a party? Enjoy herself at his expense? she thought, blotting the soft curve of her lips with a tissue. She'd been cooped up here for days. She needed to get out. See new faces. Talk to people. So why shouldn't she go?

He was sitting in the lounge thumbing through a magazine, but rose instantly as she came in, his gaze running over her with cool, masculine appreciation.

In a gown of midnight-blue satin, she knew she looked ultra-feminine and desirable, because the dress was soft and clinging, its neckline plunging sharply almost to the waist so that she had had to dispense with a bra, and with its alluring side-split from ankle to thigh, a great deal of her creamy flesh was exposed. She had shampooed her hair, too, twisting it into a thick, platinum coil from her crown to the nape of her neck, and she could tell from Elliot's unveiled admiration that her efforts pleased him.

His gaze travelled downwards, over the slender column of her throat with its silver necklace, to the generous cleft between her breasts and her pulse quickened, a warmth suffusing her cheeks—her whole body.

'You look ... unbelievably lovely ...' He seemed to catch his breath—desire holding him in thrall. But then he was moving towards her, a devastatingly male animal in dark trousers and a blue velvet dinner-jacket, back in control as he took the grey fur she was holding and placed it around her shoulders, his hands barely touching her. As if he didn't trust them to, she thought. 'Shall we go?'

Music from the mini-mansion met them half-way down the drive and Fleur experienced a sudden bout of butterflies in her stomach at the thought of meeting some of Elliot's friends.

'I gather you didn't hit it off too well with our hostess over the telephone,' he surprised her by remarking as they were ascending the steps to the front door. And when she shot him a questioning glance, wondering how he knew, he said, simply, 'Yes ... I was listening.'

She glared at him, and then tottered unsteadily, her ankle still weak, and immediately Elliot's hand was at her elbow. His touch was light, but enough to make her vibrantly aware of him, and cautiously she moved away. He probably thought she was off her head wearing three-inch heels with a sprained ankle, she decided, glancing down at her blue, strappy sandals, but she had wanted to be elegant tonight. How she wanted it! And wasn't really sure why.

'Why didn't you speak to her yourself if you were around?' she complained, remembering she had assumed him to be out when she had got up that morning.

'I heard the phone ring from the garage,' he explained, enlightening her, 'and by the time I'd got upstairs you seemed to be coping perfectly well on your own. I'm sorry if you found taking her message so tiresome,' he added, on a suddenly impatient note, 'but I wouldn't expect you to like Gaby, anyway.'

Meaning that she's a nice, well-brought up young lady, and I'm a thief, Fleur interpreted silently, and wondered why his entirely wrong assessment of her should hurt quite so much.

But he had been right about one thing. From the moment she was introduced to her hostess, Fleur knew she didn't like Gabrielle.

'And where did you find *her*?' the other woman asked him pointedly, surveying Fleur with censuring, feline-green eyes. She was petite, her bobbed hair a polished black. And without highlights, Fleur noticed, deciding that the colour had come from a bottle.

'I just happened to be there . . . so he had to bring me,' she retaliated, with a saccharine smile, and caught the flash of a warning in Elliot's eyes.

Gabrielle's narrowed, belying the curve of the bright scarlet lips which matched the clinging cat-suit she was wearing, a cool, self-assured woman Fleur put at around twenty-nine.

'How interesting,' said Gaby, touching Elliot's arm with long, painted finger-tips. 'Is that right, Elli?'

'Something like that,' he responded, laconically, as they moved nearer the loud conversation and heavy, pumping rhythm which indicated that the party was in full swing. He was looking down at the other woman, half-amused, half . . . Half what? Fleur wasn't sure. But intuition told her that Gabrielle Asquith was more to Elliot Steadman than just a friend, and for some reason it goaded. And he didn't seem too inclined to explain why he had brought another woman with him to the party either, which obviously meant he wanted to stay in his hostess's favour, Fleur concluded, with an inexplicable tug of annoyance. So why should she let him?

Lifting the heavy coil of blonde hair to flaunt the perfect column of her throat—the voluptuous beauty of her body beneath the blue satin—she murmured, with an anger-induced rashness, 'Actually, I'm his daily.'

Gabrielle's dark brows came together under the unnaturally black fringe, before Elliot said sharply, 'Fleur's found it necessary to be my guest for the past few days . . . much to our mutual regret.' This with a hard look at her as he removed her grey fur. 'Well . . . are we going in?'

That was it. No further explanations—clarifications—for the bewildered-looking Gabrielle, making it plain that men like Elliot Steadman deemed themselves unaccountable to anyone.

'There are a lot of people here *your* age,' Gabrielle emphasised, in a deprecating tone, clinging to her prize guest in a way which made Fleur embarrassed for her. 'So don't be afraid to mingle.'

'And behave yourself.'

Elliot's harsh whisper was for Fleur's ears alone so that she was hissing back, 'Don't worry . . . I shan't steal the silver.' But he had gone, totally monopolised by his beautiful hostess.

Fleur watched them merge into the circle of gyrating bodies—a dark, predatory sophisti*cat* with her chosen prey. And that description was apt, she thought, watching Gabrielle's slinky body uncoiling in Elliot's arms, hers winding around his neck with the dangerous grace of a lynx.

She swung away so that she couldn't see them
together—for some reason resenting it—and wondered
what would happen if she suddenly shouted out her
grievances to everyone—told them why she was really
here this evening. When she had threatened to expose
Elliot to his host in the car on the way over, he had said,
quite unperturbed, 'Dale's a businessman himself . . .
he'd probably applaud me if you did.' And looking at the
ruddy-faced man with the raucous laugh and bulging
midriff at the other end of the room, somehow she
guessed that she'd get no sympathy from that quarter. Or
any other, she thought glumly. Because if her weak
explanation was weighed against her employer's, it
would be him people would sympathise with, not her.

'Hel-lo.'

'The slow drawl of appreciation made her turn
sharply. A young man in a grey suit was standing behind
her, a glass of beer in one hand, a plate sporting a large
piece of gâteau in the other.

'Would you care to dance?'

Fleur couldn't contain a giggle. 'You seem to have your
hands pretty full as it is.'

Immediately, the refreshments were set aside. 'Now?'
he enquired, so eagerly, that Fleur felt cruel having to
refuse him.

'I'm sorry to be a bore but . . .' She shot a glance
downwards. 'I've got this sprained ankle . . .'

He looked disappointed. 'Well, that's not too original,
but I get the message.'

'No really, it's true.' Why was she so reluctant to see
him go? She didn't know him from Adam, even if he did
seem friendly and quite attractive. Her shoulders lifted
slightly beneath the midnight-satin. 'It's unfortunate . . .'

And suddenly she had his interest again, because he
was offering to fetch her a drink. She glanced across at
Elliot who was glowering in her direction and she had the

distinct feeling that he objected to her becoming too
friendly with anyone here tonight, so she said with a wide
smile, 'Thanks . . . I'll have a glass of medium dry white.'

He came back with something else—punch, she
thought he said it was—but she didn't feel like making a
fuss, and so she accepted it politely. In fact it was rather
nice—warm and strangely comforting—and she sat
sipping it with unusual abandon, listening to the voluble
young man at her side without really digesting a word.

She couldn't keep her eyes away from Elliot—Elliot
with his arms around Gabrielle. They were swaying to a
deep, sensual rhythm and she couldn't help thinking how
good they looked together. He, tall and tanned, that
striking sexual presence of his setting him apart from the
rest of the men in the room; the creature in his arms,
laughing and lovely—with a face and figure any woman
would envy. And as Gabrielle turned a smug smile in her
direction, Fleur was startled to realise that she was
nursing a strong desire to claw those cat-green eyes right
out of their sockets.

'You're looking very fierce.'

Her companion, drawing on a cigar, was studying her
interestedly, and Fleur had to struggle to arrange her
pale, tormented features into some semblance of composure before murmuring, 'Am I?' and trying to laugh.

But she knew she was, and she knew why. She was
jealous!—crazy though it was. Elliot Steadman hadn't
been near her since they had arrived and she was
suffering agonies of Hell because of it! In spite of herself,
she wanted to be the one in his arms—the one he smiled
at with such heart-stopping warmth—but it was clear he
despised her because of what he thought she had done,
and though she kept telling herself that she didn't care,
deep down she did.

The smoke and the noise and the over-exuberant
voices were acting like a grinding-wheel on her nerves,

and she had the vaguest suspicion that Chris—as he had
introduced himself—had been topping up her glass
without her permission, but she was past caring about
anything. The huge, Georgian room with its elaborate
ceiling, French windows and chandeliers seemed to be
closing in around her, so that all she wanted was to find
her way out of there. And hearing Chris excusing himself
to get another drink, she made to move, only to be stalled
by someone dropping down on to the vacated chair next
to hers.

'Enjoying yourself, dear?'

Gabrielle Asquith couldn't have been less interested,
and Fleur's response was curt and sarcastic. 'Immensely.'

'I'm sorry if you feel I've monopolised Elli,' the other
woman said, patronisingly, 'but you know . . . he's never
been able to help himself where I'm concerned.'

I don't believe that, thought Fleur, sourly. He probably
helped himself as often as he wanted to, and with no
complaints at all from Gabrielle Asquith!

'Funny,' Fleur remarked, suddenly finding she had
more than her usual volume of self-confidence. 'I was
under the impression it was the other way around.'

Her words hit home. The scarlet-tipped fingers
tightened around the long-stemmed glass, and for a
moment Gabrielle's knuckles showed white. Clearly, she
was struggling to keep her temper in check—and was
only just succeeding.

'There's no point in being jealous,' she purred through
her bright red lips. 'I would have thought it was obvious a
man like that would prefer a more mature woman every
time.' She lifted a rather rounded chin to gaze at the
subject of her desire who was engrossed in an exclusively
male conversation with her father, Colonel Asquith, and
several younger men on the other side of the room.
Across the bobbing heads of the dancers, Fleur could see
how eagerly those young male guests were listening to

something Elliot was saying—keen to get to know him—
as if making his acquaintance could substantially
influence their careers. Then he moved his head—caught
her watching him—and she looked away, though not
before a sharp tingle of excitement ran through her.

'I helped him decorate his new place.' Gabrielle's
proud announcement broke through Fleur's confused
emotions to assure her that here was the owner of the
earring and the dungarees. 'He's hung my housewarming
present on the main wall of his lounge, that's how much
he thinks of it,' the brunette was telling her, making
something else clear.

The painting! So that was who gave it to him. Fleur
could hardly contain the smile which was tugging at her
mouth. If only Gabrielle knew! Elliot seemed to cringe
every time he looked at it. But then he *had* hung it there,
so the other woman must be important to him for him to
decide to live with something as unpleasant as that,
mustn't she? She knew a moment's bitter resentment like
when she'd seen them dancing together, and she didn't
like the feeling.

'Exactly what is he to *you*?'

Gabrielle's blunt query caught Fleur unawares. She
picked up her glass, tried to drink, but found her mouth
wasn't quite where she thought it was, and so she put it
down again rather gingerly. After days of not eating
properly, barely sleeping, the trauma with David today,
and then virtually skipping lunch, she realised she'd been
very foolish not watching how much she had been
drinking. She felt peculiarly numb, yet wonderfully—
gloriously!—light-headed, and after the ordeal of the
past week it was a welcome respite.

'Do you really want to know?' she asked, biting her
lower lip to try to stem the sudden surge of rising
rebellion. But it was already out of control and over the
band's hard, vibrating tempo, she murmured, 'Actually,

Gabrielle ... I'm his prisoner.'

She saw the scarlet lips twitch uneasily; the long-stemmed glass suspended a few inches away from them—and there was venom trickling through her hostess's words. 'What do you mean by that?'

'I mean I'm his prisoner, Gabrielle ... his captive. His hostage! Call it what you like!' She made an extravagant gesture with her hand, almost knocking her glass over on the table, but managed to catch it in time. Why was she saying all this? she wondered, trying to reason with herself. Elliot had warned her what he would do if she didn't comply with him. She gulped at the spicy punch, trying to stop herself from blabbering on, but the words kept pouring out.

'You wouldn't believe a man like that would need to keep a woman locked up, would you?' she heard herself expressing, and suddenly realised that she was revelling in telling Gabrielle. Whatever Elliot did to her, it was worth it just to see the other woman's face. 'He's even been threatening to tie me down,' she elaborated—withholding the fact that he'd only said it out of sheer exasperation when she wasn't eating—and thought with an element of satisfaction, There, Gabrielle Asquith ... make what you can of that!

Gabrielle did. Her face had gone ashen beneath the coal-black fringe—horror-struck—and her eyes were like wide, green saucers.

'I don't wish to know that,' she breathed, in a small broken voice, and then twisted away from her chair as if she had been licked by a rabid dog.

'What have I been missing? Who's been threatening to lock you up ... your boyfriend?'

Chris was beside her again, another pint of beer in his hand.

'Hardly,' Fleur muttered, almost inaudibly, and felt

her companion's arm slip tentatively around her shoulders.

'If you were *my* girl, I'd be tempted to do the same,' he whispered, and she felt his breath against her cheek, warm—reeking of alcohol. And as he made to kiss her, suddenly she was being hauled to her feet by a hand that was firm and unyielding and had a grip like steel.

'I'm sorry, Caldridge, but the lady's going home with me.'

She didn't catch Chris's reply. Only noticed how he reddened and then seemed to diminish in size beside the other man's stature, and she faced Elliot with her eyes blazing, anger emanating from every pore as his arms encircled her body.

'Of all the . . .! You've got a nerve,' she accused, trying to tug away from him, but it was useless. His hold was far too strong. 'After the way you left me on my own all evening . . .'

'Are you complaining?' The deep voice mocked, but in spite of her anger a host of pleasurable sensations were firing through her body from the sound of it—from this long-wanted physical contact with his. 'I thought I was the one person in the world you wanted to get away from,' he taunted, softly.

'You know what I mean!' Dazed from alcohol, and even more from his touch, she realised she was in complete danger of letting him see how much his indifference to her had piqued, and when the band started up with a slow, dreamy number, she knew definitely that she couldn't stay in his arms, using her ankle as a very real excuse to get away.

'You know I'm not up to dancing,' she uttered, pulling against him,

'Then lean on me.'

The deep recommendation came as an order as the unyielding arms tightened to draw her against the hard

length of his body, and a small gasp escaped her. His
cologne was intoxicating, and she could feel the play of
muscle beneath the velvet jacket as her hands rested on
his shoulders, couldn't stop them from sliding together
behind his neck, revelling in the feel of his thick, dark
hair against her skin.

He seemed to breathe a deep, satisfied sigh. 'I told you
I had business to attend to,' he said quietly, as if
apologising for leaving her for so long. 'Now . . . what
have you been saying to Caldridge . . . and Gabrielle?'

So he had been watching her, she thought, surprised,
because when she'd looked his way during the evening,
almost without exception he'd appeared not to notice
her. But obviously he'd been keeping a close watch on
her, common-sense should have told her that.

The thick, blonde coil tilted as she lifted her young face
challengingly to the hard maturity of his, admitting in a
fey whisper, 'The truth . . . that you've been holding me
prisoner . . . threatening to tie me down.'

She gasped as his arm tightened painfully against the
small of her back.

'Wishful thinking?' His eyes were dark and heavy-
lidded, and she could feel his heart beating thunderously
next to hers. Her own pulse started to hammer crazily
and for a few moments she couldn't look away from him,
a few transient moments when every cell in her body
cried out to the total masculinity of his; when he
answered it with a fleeting touch of his lips against her
temple. Then she staggered and the spell was broken,
leaving her trembling and disconcerted as he steadied
her.

'Don't worry,' she attempted to placate him, his
narrowing grey eyes making her suddenly afraid of what
her rash behaviour might lead him to do. 'I don't think
they believed me.'

'No?' he countered, his mouth grim. 'They probably

think you've given them a very graphic description of our sex life!'

Her dark eyes became two round moons as she pretended to look shocked. 'Oh Elliot . . . I *am* sorry,' she giggled, tripping over her own feet.

A thick eyebrow lifted in disbelief. 'You're tipsy!' he accused, with an element of disapproval in the deep voice.

'No, I'm not!' she protested, indignantly, and hiccuped just to prove him right.

A cleft deepened between the dark brows. 'What have you been drinking?'

His harsh demand cut through her blurred senses, and shamefully she wondered if she had made a fool of herself with Gabrielle and Chris—and was making an even bigger fool of herself with Elliot.

'I've only had two glasses of punch,' she said, defensively, and Elliot gave a humourless laugh.

'And the rest!' He was swivelling her back to the table where she had been sitting, picked up her glass and sniffed the dregs. 'Do you know what's in that stuff?' She shook her head. 'No, well perhaps it's just as well. Come on.'

'Where are we going?'

He was urging her across the room, his hand firm at her elbow, and heads were turning in their direction.

'What will people think?' she whispered, anxiously, trying to stall him as he flung open the door to the terrace. As if she cared! It was being alone with him that was worrying her.

'From what you've been telling them they'll think I can't keep my hands off you.' His breathing was hard as he bundled her outside. She felt the blast of cold air on her bare skin and turned to go back inside, only to come up against the solid wall of Elliot's chest.

'What are you trying to do ... *hic*! Give me pneumonia?'

'Sober you up.' He had shrugged out of his jacket, was placing it over her shoulders, and she drew it around her with a deep, sensual shudder because it was warm from his body heat and had that subtle, male scent about it.

'Come on, take some deep breaths. That's right. In . . . and out.'

Complying with his instructions, she tried to ignore the fact that his strong hands were on her shoulders, and that he was so close she could feel the warmth exuding from him, because however much she was excited by him—responded to him—she had to keep reminding herself that where he was concerned she was little better than a common thief.

'Didn't you realise what you were drinking?'

'Well I knew it was strong,' she said, hating the censuring note in his voice, 'but I . . .' She put her hand to her head, feeling slightly dizzy. 'I think my glass kept being topped up . . .'

Elliot's whispered expletive made her wince. 'Just wait till I get my hands on that devil Caldridge . . . I'll make him pay for this.'

'No, Elliot please.' She reached out and touched his arm, his tangible anger making her afraid for the younger man. 'Chris wasn't to know I couldn't take it . . . and anyway, there's no harm done, is there?'

'Isn't there?' he said, churlishly, and beneath the thick, black lashes his eyes were like cold steel. Of course. She'd probably ruined his relationship with Gabrielle.

She shivered, and pulling the jacket more closely around her, went to stand by the wall overlooking the wide lawn. Beyond it a lake lay black and deep, its dark surface rippling in the wind, while above it an almost full moon was making eerie shadows of the trees, its silvery beams falling like white mist over the surrounding landscape. For a moment she thought she saw a movement down there beside the lake, and then dismissed the fancy as a trick of the light.

A soft footfall told her that Elliot had come to stand behind her.

'You'll get cold,' she murmured, forcing herself not to look at him—guilty that she had taken his coat.

'I wouldn't let it worry you,' he answered, and his tone was abrasive, scouring at her heart like sandpaper.

'I wouldn't want anyone to catch pneumonia on my account,' she returned, just as cuttingly, and turning to glare at him, added pointedly, 'Even you.'

'Well I suppose that's something to be thankful for,' he breathed, with soft sarcasm, staring up at the well-lit windows of the Georgian mansion. His dark silhouette was forceful and unyielding yet strangely, Fleur's heart constricted.

'Will Phoenix go through all right?' she asked quietly—slightly breathless—caring more than he could know.

His answer was clipped. 'Yes.' Then, 'Despite your cousin's efforts to the contrary.'

Fleur looked up at him, startled, the pain she had known since that telephone call that day etching itself on her face.

'David?' she whispered, clutching the wall behind her for support.

'Yes . . . David,' He came to stand in front of her, long legs set slightly apart. From the house the muted strains of a dreamy ballad drifted towards them. 'I know what his connection was in the whole affair,' Elliot said quietly, and she could feel his anger just below the surface, lying like a cold, impenetrable barrier between them. 'I know . . . but I want to hear it from you,' he demanded in a low voice.

Fleur gripped the wall more tightly, catching her

breath. Was he bluffing? Was it a wild guess about David to make her tell him everything—throw her own flesh and blood to the lions? She wanted him to know the truth—wanted it more than anything—but despite David's atrocity—even the way he'd refused to help her to-day—she still couldn't do it.

'Don't make me,' she implored him, a sob in her throat. And let out a small cry as Elliot suddenly reached for her, hauling her hard against him.

'Yes, damn you!' he cursed deeply into the damp gold of her hair. 'Do you love him that much that you'd consent to helping him turn his hand against all my father ... my staff ... have worked for? Against me!'

She gave a little murmur as his fingers twisted roughly in the thick, gold coil but his other arm was holding her against him and she found herself battling not only with her misery, but with a mounting sexual tension on top of it.

'It wasn't like that!' she cried out in anguish—frustration—and realised, even before she had said it, that she had already admitted David's guilt. She looked at the tower of granite in front of her, at the sweep of dark hair, ruffled by the wind and falling across his brow, at the taut, hard lines of his mouth and jaw, and she staggered weakly, dropping her head against his shoulder to hide the tears which were threatening to overwhelm her. 'Oh Elliot. I didn't know,' she murmured on a shuddering sob. 'Really I didn't know...'

She didn't know whether he believed her, either. Probably not, she decided. But his arms were around her and she was clinging to him, feeling like a small child—warm, protected and safe. For a long moment they stood like that, her head resting on the broad width of his shoulder, his arms clasping her tightly to him, but suddenly he was moving to hold her away from him.

'If you're mourning lost loyalty to your cousin,' he said,

icily, aware of her tears, 'then forget it. You didn't tell me anything I didn't already know.' And when she looked at him, mouth trembling, her dark eyes questioning his as to how he knew, he said, simply, without an ounce of compunction, 'I dismissed him this afternoon.'

'You what?' Weak, breathless, she stared at him, her full lips parted slightly, a few strands of hair which had come loose from the coil blowing across her temple.

'I've suspected him ever since I took the chairmanship.' Elliot's words were quietly harsh. 'Why do you suppose he didn't get that directorship? He was management material.'

'How ... how did you find out?' she gulped, going weak at the knees.

'I'm not a fool, Fleur, and it's a sorry man ... or woman,' he expanded, making her stomach churn, 'who makes the mistake of thinking otherwise. It was only a question of having Markham watched. He had to slip up sooner or later. And when I caught you in possession of that password and your cousin didn't show up for work the following day, I knew he had to be involved. I went round to his flat to have it out with him there and then but he wasn't there,' and with a sceptical grunt, 'or pretending not to be! So I asked Andrew Moreton to bleep me the instant Markham showed his face at the office ... which he did at lunchtime today ... presumably in the hope of removing all his belongings without anyone seeing him and then doing a moonlight flit!'

Fleur swallowed, hurting inside. So David must have left his flat straight after she'd telephoned him, knowing that Elliot was with *her*, she thought, agonised by the knowledge she still couldn't accept, that her cousin could have abandoned her like that. But obviously he hadn't taken into account just how shrewd his employer was.

'Did ... did he say anything about me?' she ventured,

feeling sick, because if he hadn't, then she'd never be able to prove her innocence to Elliot, and for some reason that mattered as much as not losing her job and her reputation.

'Why didn't you come to me in the begining . . . three days ago . . . and tell me the truth?' he demanded, not answering her question, and his strong features looked strained. 'Why didn't you tell me it was David who gave you that information?'

'Would you have betrayed someone you loved?' she asked him, tears trembling on her lower lids, so wrapped up in her own misery that she didn't notice Elliot's sharp intake of breath.

'You could have saved us both a lot of trouble if you'd had the sense to tell me the truth . . . that you weren't involved and didn't know a damn thing about Phoenix until I came in and accused you.'

'I tried!' she shot back, 'but you wouldn't list . . .' She stopped short, realisation suddenly dawning. 'How did you . . .' She paused again, gulping hard. 'David?' she queried, her mind clamouring with hope.

Elliot nodded, briefly. 'He told me everything . . . eventually. But not until I virtually threatened to knock it out of him.' His eyes were burning like twin coals and inwardly Fleur recoiled. Yes, David would have succumbed under pressure like that. He'd never had the strongest of stomachs for physical violence. 'He also owned up to the other leakages we've had over the past year . . . all for a nice fat cheque from our competitors,' Elliot was saying, adding, almost as an afterthought, 'Oh . . . and he exonerated you completely.'

She gave a low, involuntary groan. Relief coursed through her, so weakening, that she would have collapsed if Elliot hadn't caught her.

Oh David! So in the end he hadn't abandoned her entirely. She could have sobbed. Dazed with relief—and from drinking too much, she suspected—her senses only partially registered the music and the laughter coming from the house. But she was suddenly very much aware of those strong arms around her, the warmth of Elliot's body next to hers and that fresh, tangy scent of him which was as familiar to her as his signature. She remembered the times he had kissed her in anger—found that she was craving for him to kiss her with tenderness now—and she felt his arms tighten around her as though in acknowledgment of her silent plea. His lips brushed a sensual caress across her hair, filling her with wanting, and she thought of how much she had wanted him in that restaurant before that bleeped summons and that hectic race through town—before those nauseating moments in his office that afternoon . . .

That *afternoon*! Suddenly life was pumping back into her veins driven by a piston of indescribable anger.

'You bastard!' Burning with rage, she flung out her arms and pushed herself away from him, coming up sharply against the wall. 'You knew! You've known since lunchtime . . . and you still let me think . . .' Anger stalled her. Her mind was swimming with a thousand unspeakable adjectives she wanted to hurl at him, her eyes flashing a sudden warning as he started towards her. 'Don't you touch me!'

She gave a tiny, guttural cry as he caught the hand she would have raised against him, his hard fingers encircling her wrist, restraining her.

'You like me touching you,' he reminded her cruelly, and beneath the yards of blue satin, she tensed, knowing that he was right.

'You could have taken me home this afternoon,' she said in a small, tight voice, and saw his mouth harden.

'I could have,' he breathed, 'but I was angry with you dammit!' His chest lifted heavily beneath the white shirt. 'Your precious David might have ruined the whole wretched deal and you'd have sat back and let it happen!'

'No!' she protested, pulling free from him. 'I wanted to ring him but you wouldn't let me. And I wasn't going to tell you a thing while you were being so damn pig-headed! Anyway, I thought . . .' She lowered her gaze, fixing it on his black shoes. 'I thought perhaps somebody on the Board had given him that password and that he'd asked me to get the information when everyone had gone because he didn't want to risk you finding out that he'd got behind with his work again. When I found out the truth I tried to persuade him to tell you himself . . . but he wouldn't agree to it. But I knew he couldn't ruin things for you,' she put in quickly, 'because he said he still needed that information . . .'

'Oh?' Elliot's tall frame moved closer to her, a hard question burning in his eyes. Of course he didn't know.

'There was a telephone in the pub,' she admitted, swallowing as she met the dark strength of his features. And suffering pangs of conscience as she had been all day over the way she had got herself out of the mews, she said, penitently, 'I got you to take me out under false pretences this morning.'

For a second his thick brows drew together, and then he said on a ragged breath, 'Yes, I suspected that.' He lifted his hand to brush a strand of blonde hair from the side of her neck, but his fingers lingered too long against the small throbbing pulse and its quickening betrayed her. He caught her chin, tilting her face to his, and she thought how smug he must feel, aware of this uncontrollable response in her, although he didn't look smug. The line of his mouth was relaxed—almost tender—and the cleft between his brows had deepened, lending him an expression not dissimilar to pain.

'Fleur . . .'

He didn't finish. A shrill scream split the silence of the darkness beyond the terrace, followed by a violent splash

RUDE AWAKENING 117

as something hit the surface of the water. Fleur's eyes
followed Elliot's swift glance lakewards, but a cloud was
blotting out the moonlight and she could see nothing.
Then the screaming came again—feminine and fran-
tic—and someone else was yelling, 'Help! For God's
sake, somebody help!'

Fleur's blood ran cold. She shot a startled look at
Elliot, but already he was twisting away from her,
running with an animal's sure agility down the terrace
steps towards the lake. She tried to follow, but couldn't
run in her high-heeled sandals, so she took them off,
wincing as the wetness of the grass saturated her feet, the
cold seeming to penetrate her bones. From halfway
across the lawn she saw Elliot's outline as he plunged into
the murky, green water and she shuddered, praying
silently, please, let it be all right.

She was standing at the water's edge when he emerged,
soaked to the skin, and watched helplessly as he waded
up the deep shelf of mud with the inert figure of a girl in
his arms. A youth was scrambling up after him, drenched
and distraught.

'I don't know how it happened,' the boy wailed,
virtually in tears as he came up to Fleur. 'We were out
there in the boat and it just capsized!'

'It'll be all right,' she murmured, reassuringly, placing
a comforting hand on his sleeve, but as she caught the
look of grave concern on Elliot's face, suddenly she
wasn't so certain. The girl had been out in the middle of
the lake so that it had taken precious moments for him to
reach her, and now she lay without uttering a sound, her
arms hanging limply on either side of her.

Fleur's heart seemed to stop. She couldn't move. But
Elliot wasn't wasting a second. Laying the girl face
downwards on the grass, he adjusted her arms above her
head—elbows at an angle from her body—and began
easing them back and forth with steady, rhythmic

movements, using all his surprising know-how to pump the water out of her lungs.

He shot a quick glance up at the youth. 'Well don't just stand there lad . . . go and get a warm blanket. And get out of those wet clothes as quickly as you can.'

The urgent authority in his voice motivated the youth so that he raced off at once, and still Elliot kept pumping.

'Come on!' He gave an anguished growl and Fleur looked at him in horror, fearing the worst. But suddenly the girl made a sound—something between a vomit and a cough—and started to move.

Fleur looked at Elliot, caught his smile of intense relief, and knew such overwhelming relief herself she almost wanted to laugh.

'Is there anything I can do?' she asked quickly, feeling totally helpless. He had just saved a life and all she had done was stood by and watched!

'We'll have to get her out of these wet clothes before she catches her death,' he said, concerned, because the girl was starting to shiver, and lifting her into his arms again, he began striding briskly back to the house.

Following, Fleur's heart went out to him in a surge of anxiety and some other emotion she didn't even begin to question at that moment. Water was trickling down his face from his dark hair which was flattened against his head, and his clothes were clinging to him, the silk shirt transparent against his broad back. In the light of the now unhindered moon, she thought she saw him shiver, too.

'Would you like your jacket?' she offered, anxiously, feeling totally useless again, as well as breathless from trying to keep pace with him.

'Keep it on,' he ordered, when she made to remove it from her own shoulders, and he pulled a wry face when he saw the sandals dangling from her hands, noticed her bare feet. 'You should have gone back to the house

instead of chasing after me like that,' he admonished, but
softly, and from the absent smile which flitted across his
lips she knew that he was grateful for her moral support.
All her anger towards him had gone, she realised, shaken
out of her by what had just happened—what he had
done—and she couldn't explain the emotions which were
washing over her—didn't want to—intent only on
keeping up with Elliot's long strides. Her ankle protested
miserably, but she forced all thought of pain aside. After
all, what was a sprained ankle against someone's life?

The girl was whimpering, probably from fright as well
as cold, Fleur guessed, and as they climbed the steps,
people were filtering out on to the terrace, informed of
what had happened, no doubt, by the girl's boyfriend.

'What happened?'

'Is she all right?'

'Who is it?'

Urgent questions which went unanswered by Elliot as
he elbowed his way through a sea of curious faces to find
Gabrielle.

It didn't take him long. She was coming downstairs
with the blanket he had requested from the youth, and
though she had been prepared for what Elliot was
bringing her, she still had to press scarlet-tipped fingers
to her lips to stem her cry of horror at the sight of her
unfortunate young guest.

'Get her undressed and into a hot bath immediately,'
he instructed, and Gabrielle obeyed, and then to Fleur's
surprise, asked if she would help. Fleur complied,
realising afterwards that her assistance had been
required not because her hostess wanted her company—
because the other woman barely spoke two words to
her—but because Gabrielle was obviously disinclined to
deal with the overwrought teenager on her own! Fleur
was only too happy to help, since attending to the girl's
needs kept her own worries at bay, but later, when Elliot

was driving her back to her flat, they came crowding in
around her.

What was going to happen about her job? Was he
going to dismiss her? Really, she supposed, he would be
quite justified in doing so after the way she had withheld
relevant facts from him. And what about David? Would
he wind up in prison? She shuddered, and with a
sickening pain in her stomach, managed to ask, 'Are you
taking David to court?'

'No.' She glanced at him, surprised by his very
decisive reply, but he was looking at the road—at the
cats' eyes coming interminably towards them through
the darkness. They reminded her of Gabrielle.

'Dragging him through the courts won't do any of us
any good,' he expressed, thrusting the Jaguar into a lower
gear to take a bend. 'We can do without that sort of bad
publicity . . . and I'm sure Markham will have learned his
lesson . . . if a type like that ever does! He's hardly likely
to find himself a responsible position in this country
again.'

No, Fleur thought. You'll probably see to that. But
nevertheless, she had to close her eyes against the tears of
immense relief that her cousin was going to be let off so
lightly. After all, he did deserve worse.

'And me,' she ventured, tremulously, across the car's
dark interior. 'Would you prefer it if I handed in my own
resignation, or do you want the satisfaction of firing me
yourself?'

Obviously he hadn't made up his mind about that as he
didn't answer immediately. He switched on the wind
screen wipers because it had started to rain, and she
looked at him from under her lashes, wondering what he
was thinking. He had showered at Gabrielle's and his
hair was still slightly damp, the dry clothes he had
borrowed from Colonel Asquith left at the mews and
substituted for his own when they had stopped there to

collect Fleur's few belongings. Now he was wearing a
light shirt and trousers, his leather jacket thrown casually
over the top.

'Is that what you want?' His voice was emotionless—
his eyes still on the road—but then he swore softly, letting
out a deep breath. 'You're a damn good programmer,
Fleur Galaway . . . an essential part of my staff, so unless
you have other ideas . . .' He glanced her way, his mouth
curling wryly, 'like pressing charges for abduction for
instance . . . I'd like you back in the office as soon as
possible.'

As he pulled up outside of her flat, Fleur tried to digest
what he had just said. He wanted her back in the office?
It hardly seemed credible! But did she want that?
Earlier, in *his* office she'd made up her mind that she
didn't, but even before she had asked herself the
question, she knew that deep down she did. And now
that she knew David wasn't going to be prosecuted, most
of her anxieties were ebbing away. All that was left was a
deep core of unhappiness that her own cousin could have
done what he did, together with a small, nagging worry
about how she would cope with the office gossip when
everyone found out why he had been dismissed. But she
would have to face that when the time came. 'Thank
you,' she said, quietly, sadly.

'He really wasn't worth all your loyalty, was he?' Elliot
returned, seeming, in that uncanny way of his, to know
what she was thinking. And more aggressively, the truth
of his words stabbing her like a knife, 'He didn't give a
damn about you.'

'That's different,' she whispered, desolately, trying to
look for some justification for the way David had treated
her. 'He was probably afraid . . .'

'And you weren't?' Elliot was tilting her face towards
his, his thumb flicking over the soft pout of her lower lip.
'Aren't you afraid of me, Fleur?'

She trembled, her heart starting to thud, and she looked at the hard angles of his face—the rigid set of his mouth and strong, thrusting jaw—managing to keep her voice steady as she answered, 'No.'

And that sounded like a challenge, she thought, silently criticising her rashness, because she was afraid. Afraid of this dangerous, sexual influence he could exert over her. So, for her own self-preservation, she added, 'Well . . . not really.'

A dark eyebrow lifted in amusement. He knew exactly why she had been quick to amend that.

'I think . . . not at all,' he said, laughing softly as he reached to uncoil the heavy, gold twist of her hair. 'I'm inclined to think it's your own response to me that you're afraid of.'

'No!' Panicking, she pushed against him as he bent to take her mouth with his own, but she was no match for him and he got his way, delving into the depths of her soul as his tongue probed between the sweet honey of her lips. She was yielding to his kiss, desire melting her blood to liquid gold, flooding her body with fire and warmth and sensation. His hand had slid inside the deep vee of her dress and she gasped as it closed over her breast, moulding it to his warm palm. She strained against him, desire tingling through every nerve, arching her body in response to his coaxing hands and entwining her fingers in his strong hair, murmuring his name.

'Oh Fleur,' he groaned, lifting his head to gaze down upon her pliant body, seeing her creamy breast exposed, the nipple round and full, her eyes heavy-lidded and her mouth swollen from his kiss. 'Whether people thought it tonight . . . it's true,' he whispered heavily. 'I can't keep my hands off you.' And proved it by sliding them down over her narrow waist to the deep bowl of her hips, then upwards again to gather her to him. She could feel how aroused he was. His body was taut and trembling, And as her hands moved over the soft leather of his jacket, she heard him groan in a deep agony of need.

His lips were inflicting sweet torture on the sensitive column of her neck, nipping the soft flesh, sending a sensual message through her body to the very core of her femininity. Somehow she had unbuttoned his shirt, was running her hands over the mat of thick, wiry hair and, as she became more daring, followed the path of her urgent fingers with her tongue. He gave another deep groan, then another which sounded almost angry, his mouth covering hers now with a fierce desperation as he pushed her back against the seat. But when she would have caught him to her, craving the weight of his body on hers, he drew away from her, taking her hand and pressing it, palm upwards, to his lips.

'No,' he said, gently firm. 'I've never yet taken advantage of a woman who has had too much to drink ... and I don't propose doing it now.'

'Oh please ...' The small, broken cry escaped her as his dark, rising profile confirmed his intention to get out of the car, and mindless, she caught at his sleeve, her body so racked with wanting that pride deserted her. 'I'm not drunk,' she whispered, in a small appeal to him.

'No?' He gave her a lopsided smile. Bent to kiss the tip of her nose and then the swollen peak of her breast which brought her straininq towards him for more, and left her desolate ad cold when he didn't comply. 'Perhaps not now,' he agreed, his emotions back under strict control again. 'but you certainly weren't responsible for your actions an hour ago.'

He was probably right. But it goaded to have the fact pointed out to her, especially as she'd always avoided strong alcohol like the plague, and she felt thoroughly ashamed. But what was worse—humiliating!—was the way she had shown him how much she had wanted him—whether because of it or not—and then suffered the mortification of being rejected. She felt like a child who had been reprimanded and then denied a special treat, and as Elliot came round to open her door for her, she said tartly, an agitated flush to her cheeks, 'I'm sorry if I showed you up in front of your friends.'

'They're Gabrielle's friends . . . not mine,' he replied, laconically, but she was still feeling too ashamed of herself to query the weary note in his voice, and as they reached her front door, he said, misunderstanding her despondency, 'Stop feeling so sorry for yourself. Most people let themselves go once in a while.' He turned her to face him and she thought how exhausted he looked. There were tired lines around his eyes—dark smudges beneath them—but then it had been an exacting night. 'If you hadn't had a little too much to drink tonight we wouldn't have been on that terrace . . . and if we hadn't, that poor unfortunate girl would most certainly have drowned.'

The startling truth of that statement didn't register with her until much later. At that moment she was alive only to the fleeting touch of his lips on hers. And then he was gone, leaving her with a sudden, deep ache in her loins from the memory of his lovemaking, and the cold, nagging suspicion that he had halted it because of Gabrielle.

CHAPTER SEVEN

'I don't know what's wrong with Elliot.' The redheaded telephonist perched herself on the corner of Fleur's desk, wriggling to pull the tight, black leather skirt down over her thighs. 'Ever since he moved house he's been like a bear with a sore head!'

Silently, Fleur agreed, sipping the cup of coffee Trudy had brought up for her, her heart seeming to give a little twist. Elliot Steadman had barely spoken to her since dropping her off at her flat last Thursday. He had been busy finalising the Phoenix deal—she knew that—a multi-million pound contract with an international group of companies all because of a component which could revolutionise micro-technology! Everyone knew about it now. But although matters had been concluded without a hitch, Elliot's hard, driving demands whilst negotiations had been under way had now lapsed into a deep, brooding silence. And that he was intent on avoiding Fleur was obvious. She had only seen him briefly since her return to work; once when he was shooting off to play squash during the lunch-hour and she had almost collided with him coming out of the lift; and once or twice when he had swept into her office to check over some accounts, but on each occasion he had shown her no more than an employer's cool courtesy towards an employee. He'd had her surrender, she thought, miserably—the memory of that night in his car still able to bring a flush to her cheeks—even though he hadn't acted upon it, and his desire to have nothing more to do with her couldn't have been more plain if he had spelt it out in writing.

'By the way . . . what's David doing?' Trudy Marshall's question shook her violently back to the present.

'I don't know,' she murmured, and noticing that her calendar still showed the previous month, got up to adjust it. The fresh print was an Impressionist work, its vivid oranges and reds quite out of sympathy with her unhappy state of mind. 'He said he was going to see someone about a job in Liverpool.' Or perhaps he was already in Liverpool, she ruminated, sitting down again, because he wasn't at the flat. And the only time she had spoken to him had been when she'd telephoned him last Friday before coming into the office, and she'd been so livid with him then because of what he'd done, she hadn't taken in a word he'd said about his future plans.

'Fancy getting into a row with Elliot and walking out like that,' the other girl remarked, finishing the dregs of her coffee. 'He should have known better than to cross our lord and master!'

'Yes,' Fleur responded flatly, relieved that Trudy—or anyone else at Steadman's for that matter, other than Board members—didn't know the full facts behind David's leaving the firm. At least that was one thing in Elliot's favour, she thought, silently grateful to him, because he had called for full discretion in the matter among his top management, and she strongly suspected that his decision had been made solely to make her position in the office less stressful.

'He's probably cooked his chances of getting a reference from that beautiful animal upstairs, hasn't he?' Trudy sympathised, fluffing up her short, red curls with painted fingertips. 'I wouldn't like to get on the wrong side of that man's temper . . . although I must confess I think he looks ever so sexy when he's wild!' She picked up the small, white plastic cup and grimaced at its lack of contents. 'Do you know . . . he even remarked yesterday that if I spent less time drinking coffee and more time taking calls, company sales would increase by five per cent!'

'The sarcastic devil!' Fleur exhaled, straightening the collar of her white blouse, although to be honest with herself she had to acknowledge that Elliot did have a point. It didn't take much to seduce Trudy away from the switchboard. Nevertheless, she didn't feel like siding with her employer. His total indifference towards her was causing her inexplicable pain, so that wounded pride had her answering with an unnaturally sharp edge to her tongue. 'He's just plain arrogant, overbearing and . . . and he'd probably be more in his element if he could wield a whip!'

'Ummm,' the redhead approved with a sensually inspired shudder. Then with a sudden grimace at Fleur, slid off the desk and scuttled quickly away. And Fleur realised why. The subject of their discussion was standing in the doorway.

'Turner?' He had moved over to the calendar—was studying the new month's print—and she recognised a small tug of satisfaction in replying.

'Monet, actually.'

Closer inspection confirmed it, and he nodded. 'But very influenced by the Turner technique . . . even though Monet might have denied it himself.'

'Did he?' She glanced up interestedly. Met a gaze that was far too disturbing and had to look away again. And with a struggle for equanimity, added, 'I sometimes confuse him with Pissarro.'

He gave her a half-smile. 'Not an unforgivable mistake. I believe their careers were closely interwined.' And moving nearer to her, 'What I actually came down for was an analysis of the breakdown of the last quarter's figures . . .' He was simply the Chairman again— company business uppermost—and with a deep ache somewhere around her heart, Fleur put the computer into operation.

'Shall I bring it up?' she suggested, almost as an entreaty, because the sight of his dark-suited figure was making her pulses work overtime and she knew she wouldn't settle until he'd gone.

'No ... I want to see if we can approach it in a different way ... get more information out of this thing.'

He was going to stay there! Heart thumping, Fleur didn't know how she was going to work with him beside her, not without making a complete fool of herself anyway. Her fingers were already trembling on the keys!

'What sort of thing did you have in mind?' She was so breathless her voice was shaking, but he seemed quite oblivious to the havoc he was creating inside her, casually pulling up a chair to sit down.

'Something like this ...' She caught a waft of lemony aftershave, and as he leaned across to tap in the new information, his arm accidentally brushed her shoulder, sending a sharp tingle through her body. She felt hot and sticky. How could she concentrate with him so close? she wondered, distractedly, fingering her neat chignon in a small, nervous gesture. But it was her job, and she knew she had to, exercising all the control she could muster as she analysed his proposed system on the computer's screen.

'No, that won't work,' she advised, suddenly forgetting everything but the important matter in hand.

'Oh?' The cool, grey eyes looked amused. 'All right ... show me a better way.'

It was a challenge she couldn't resist. Proficiently, she began to tap out an amendment to his program, sending him an occasional glance to see if he approved. He leaned closer, his dark gaze intent as he scanned the visual display, his strong, handsome features totally absorbed.

'Good God! I think you've made a breakthrough!' His

deep laugh made the other two girls in the office look up interestedly, and he gave Fleur an impressed smile which caused her heart to flip. 'Show me how it works in practice.'

She complied, basking in the warmth of his approval—his attention, however impersonal—enjoying working with him.

Intellectually, he stimulated her as no one else could. It was this rapport they shared through their work which had attracted her to him in the first place—apart from that undeniable charisma—and during the days that followed it seemed to strengthen, growing from a common interest in facts and figures, to flourish in lengthy, vivifying discussions, their often animated exchanges drawing envious glances from Stacey and June. But their discussions seldom stretched beyond company affairs, and Elliot's apparent aims to keep their relationship on a purely business level only served to assure Fleur of his uninterest in her as a person. He had had her capitulation that night in the car, and she wondered if that had been enough to satisfy his dominant male ego—wondered even if his obvious desire for her at the mews had been induced solely by his anger, so that after procuring her surrender—and therefore her humiliation in refusing her—she was no longer a challenge to him sexually.

She shuddered, convincing herself that she was right—that beyond their working harmony he felt only contempt for her, which brought about more humiliation—more pain. She began to lose her appetite—and sleep. As far as her days were stimulating, her nights were miserable, and she went to bed each evening only to wake in the early hours, sobbing and perspiring and alone. The nightmares had taken on a vivid, new concept. She was still trapped, but in a murky, green sea of her own misery, a sea in which she swam frantically

for the shoreline and never made it, her efforts impeded
by lots of floating, clanging triangles all joined together.
They became tangled in her hair, through her fingers,
clinging mercilessly to her slender ankles, and there was
a boat, too, bobbing about on the dingy, green surface,
drifting with no one on board, save for an agile, clawing
black cat which spat and snarled at her whenever she
swam near.

She turned restlessly in bed, her waking brain scoffing
the ridiculous imagery of her subconscious, but try
though she did, she could not so easily dismiss thoughts
of Elliot, or the way in which she had offered herself so
shamelessly to him that night. Eventually, when her
sleepless nights began to tell in the dark smudges beneath
her eyes, and particularly when she knew her work was
starting to suffer, she decided she would have to get away
from Elliot Steadman before she went insane.

Consequently, she arrived at the office early one
morning before he came in, and left her typewritten
notice on his desk, placing it on his blotter so that it
would be the first thing he saw when he sat down. And
then she spent the morning on tenterhooks, waiting for a
summons which never came. After lunch when there was
still no response from him, she decided that she must
have picked a day when he wasn't coming in. Her jittery
nerves began to relax as she became certain of it, and she
was just buzzing Trudy for confirmation of the fact when
June, the young blonde typist, called from across the
room,

'Hey, Fleur! Our illustrious leader just rang through on
my line. He wants to see you in his office.'

So this was it! The final confrontation.

In the lift which bore her up to the executive suite,
Fleur ran her hands nervously over her soft chignon, then
down over the fitted, beige skirt she had worn to
complement the coffee-silk of her blouse, wondering

what Elliot would say. Would he be surprised? Shocked? Angry perhaps? Surely he'd show some emotion now other than the torturous politeness he'd been showing her for the past couple of weeks?

He was sitting at his desk, dark head bent in concentration, but he stood up as she entered, his manners impeccable as always.

'Have a seat.' He gestured casually to the chair facing his own and she complied gratefully, because her legs were already weakening at the sight of him.

He was wearing a dark blue shirt with grey suit trousers, his jacket discarded over the back of his chair, and he looked relaxed, in spite of that air of command. Too relaxed, Fleur thought, with a sudden tightening of her stomach muscles.

He deposited himself on one corner of his desk—the grey fabric stretching tight across his thigh—and slapped the piece of paper he was holding. 'I take it you're serious about this?'

Fleur swallowed, and answered, resolutely, 'Yes.' She hadn't got up in the early hours and typed that notice for nothing!

Elliot rose and came to stand immediately in front of her, his grey eyes darkened by the deep colour of his shirt, seeming to plumb the depths of hers. A line deepened on his tanned forehead and Fleur's heart took an unexpected leap. Was he wanting her to stay?

'Is there anything I can do to make you change your mind?' he said, so that raging hope coursed through her. 'Good programmers like you are very difficult to replace.'

She should have known. He was only concerned with the continuing efficiency of his company.

'No,' she delivered, bluntly, a spark of anger hiding the hurt in her dark eyes.

For a long moment his gaze rested on her face, and she swallowed again, unable to look away. He had the power to sap the strength out of her with just one look, and he was doing it right now.

'Are you still having nightmares?'

Fleur blinked hard, startled by the sudden change of subject and the softness of his voice; then silently reproached herself for not having worn her hair loose. Such a severe style as the chignon emphasised the dark shadows around her eyes—the pallor of her thin cheeks—and that too-keen perception of Elliot's had made him wise to them at once.

'No,' she bluffed, colouring, feeling as though she were exchanging confidences with a doctor rather than the Chairman of the Board. 'They're all cleared up now.'

He nodded briefly. 'What are you going to do? Have you got another job?'

Even for her own sake, she couldn't go on lying to him, and she shook her head. 'I might go abroad,' she said, having given some thought to that idea and not rejecting it entirely.

The hard mouth seemed to tighten and he went back to his chair, studying her notice again. He must have read dozens in his time, she thought. It was all part of being the head of a thriving business. And she waited with bated breath for him to say something, searching her mind for a good reason to refuse him if he asked her to stay on again.

'I think it's probably for the best.' His unexpected comment brought her startled eyes to his—cool and frank and unrelenting—and through a haze of unreality she realised that he fully intended to let her go. 'I can understand how you must feel . . .'

Did he? In a daze she heard him offering his regrets—a spill of well-rehearsed words and phrases he must have played out on his stage of authority in countless

performances, to countless employees before her—but
why did it hurt so much?

'If you feel you'd like to go this afternoon . . .' He took
an envelope out of his desk drawer. 'I can probably
arrange for someone to fill in until we get another full-
time operator . . . and I'll have your salary made up for a
full month.'

He was suggesting that she go straight away? She had
asked him in her note if he would waive the full month's
notice required, allowing her to leave sooner if he found
someone else in the meantime, but he'd not only agreed
to it, he couldn't wait to get rid of her! Pain clawed at her
heart and it took all her will-power to pull her features
into calm, composed lines, her hair a shining halo above
her throbbing temples. After all, it was what she wanted,
wasn't it?

'Thank you,' she murmured, numbly, reaching for the
envelope containing her cards and personal papers, and
flinched as his bronzed hand casually brushed hers.

Hurt, angry, she jumped up, wanting to get away from
him as quickly as she could. But he had followed her to
the door and, fingers on the handle, he seemed to hesitate
before opening it.

'You'll be all right?' It was there again, that odd
inflexion in his voice, and Fleur nodded, unbelievably
choked. He was too near, that subtle, male scent of him
so disturbingly familiar that she had an almost overwhelming compulsion to turn to him—to touch him—
was afraid of what she would do if he touched her. But he
was already opening the door.

'There'll be no problem about a reference . . .' He was
the employer again, all traces of emotion gone, and with
a smile pasted on her lips Fleur thanked him mechanical-
ly, walking away, numb from the knowledge that she
would probably never see him again.

The warmth of the cottage struck her as soon as she opened the front door. She knew that the farmer's wife, the nearest neighbour over half a mile away, came in occasionally to give the place an airing—that was a permanent arrangement, but the atmosphere was almost lived in, homely, just like those weekends when she used to come down here to Cornwall when her aunt was alive. Impatiently she brushed at the tears which sprang unwittingly to her eyes. Having needed to get away for a while after leaving Steadman's that afternoon, there was nothing in the world she wanted more at that moment than her aunt's ample bosom to cry on.

But Aunt Aggie was dead, she told herself firmly, dumping her case on to the living-room table, and she had to sort out her problems on her own.

Strangely, everything looked the same as it always had. The plates on the mantelpiece over the fireplace. The two easy chairs beside it. The oak dresser against the far wall displaying all her aunt's antique china. But the stranger thing was that familiar smell of burning apple-wood . . .

Moving over to the hearth she could see why. There were ashes—fresh ashes—in the grate. Before she could grasp the reason for it, she was swinging round, startled, as the front door suddenly burst open.

'David!'

When he saw her he dropped several of the logs he had been carrying, swearing as one landed on his foot.

'Hell . . . Fleur! What are you doing here? You're the last person I expected to see.'

'It's all right,' she shot back bitterly, 'I shan't be staying!' Piqued at seeing him there, she swung her suitcase up and made to brush past him, but a hand descended on her arm, stopping her dead.

'Don't be silly. I know you said you never wanted to see me again when you rang last week . . . but I didn't think you meant it seriously.'

'Well I did!' Dropping her suitcase, she looked at him hard, at his thick, blond hair; his untidy sweater and jeans. And suddenly she was crying, sobbing for the time when she was a child and he a teenager fetching logs for his mother—for the days before everything changed. She felt his hand lightly touch her shoulder. And then he was striding away from her—dropping logs down on to the hearth with a heavy thud. He was the same old David, she thought. Never over-abundant with comfort. Never knowing what to do when someone cried. And she remembered how sometimes she'd seen Aunt Aggie break her heart over flaws in her son's character—flaws which she, Fleur, couldn't see at the time. His obsession with making money; the importance he placed on material things; the way he had sometimes trodden on others in his way to the top—things which she hadn't seen then but which came to her so vividly now.

'Why did you do it?' she sobbed, facing him, one thick plait draped like a silver robe over her shoulder. 'You had a good job with Steadman's . . .'

'Oh don't let's go into *that* again!' He swung round, impatient, his hands on his hips, a thin smear of mud from his boots on the rug behind him. 'I told you over the phone . . . I did it for me . . . number one.' He pointed an angry thumb towards his chest. 'Steadman's didn't worry about *me* . . . especially that Elliot. Why d'you suppose I didn't get that promotion?'

'Because he *knew*!' she fired at him, dark eyes blazing in the soft pallor of her face. 'He knew all along what you were doing! He just needed proof that was all!'

'Which *you* gave him.'

The accusation stung. 'No!' She turned away from him towards the window. Somewhere out there was the Atlantic Ocean—the familiar rugged cliffs—only she couldn't see it because it was so dark. 'I didn't tell him,

David,' she said more subduedly, sadly. 'Not until he'd
dismissed you, anyway. He worked it all out for himself.'

'How could he have? No one's *that* shrewd.' His lips
twisted in positive hatred. He'd never liked Elliot, she
thought, and suspected that it was mainly because he *was*
shrewd. Shrewd and successful and rich—everything
David wanted to be himself and hadn't quite succeeded
in being.

'I must admit . . . he did say you hadn't told him
anything,' he amazed her by saying as he began
shovelling up the ashes, 'and all I can say to that is that
you must be a lot stronger than you look. And at this
moment you look just about all in.' She noticed a tinge of
sympathy in his clear, blue eyes as they studied her. 'Did
he give you a hard time, kid?'

Sending him a scathing glance as an answer she felt
him watching her as she shrugged out of her anorak.
When she turned round his gaze was running over her
soft contours beneath the warm, cashmere sweater, tight
denims and long, black boots, and his eyes suddenly
narrowed.

'He didn't . . .'

'Oh David! For Heaven's sake!' She knew what his
thoughts were and found them more than a little
embarrassing, stuffing her hands as far as she could get
them into the pockets of her tight jeans. 'I'm a big girl
now.'

'So I've only just realised.' David pulled a wry
expression. 'And from the rumours I've heard about
Steadman he's never without one in his bed!'

Flushing, Fleur turned away to stare at her aunt's
small, framed sampler on the opposite wall, flinching
when David remarked, 'I wouldn't exactly say you were
his sophisticated type, cousin dear . . . but you've
certainly got all the right equipment. Are you sure he . . .'

'No!' She swung back to face him, colour spreading

like a bright flame across her cheeks. 'I'm quite able to take care of myself, thank you!' she retorted hotly. If only David knew! She could take care of herself all right! If it hadn't been for Elliot's immense self-control that last night, she thought ashamedly, they might well have ended up in *her* bed! 'I'll make some coffee,' she said, needing to get out of the room.

When she came back with two steaming mugs, a fire was just leaping to life in the grate.

'I've sold the car,' David said, explaining why she hadn't seen his vehicle outside. He sat down opposite her at the table. 'I'm emigrating . . . going to Australia.'

'Australia?' Fleur breathed in shock. 'What are you going to do there? The same sort of thing you were doing here?'

David grimaced, gulping his coffee thirstily. 'Hardly. Big game fishing . . . that's where the money lies. No more white-collar work for me. I'll show Steadman he can't break me . . . reference or no reference!' This with a degree of malice. 'No . . . Josh and me . . . that's the chap I went to see in Liverpool . . . we're flying out on the twenty-ninth of this month. Then . . .' He snapped his fingers in the air with a self-satisfied smile. 'Those big game devils aren't going to know what hit them!'

Absently, Fleur put her mug down and stared at him. 'But you don't even like fish!' she cried, incredulously. 'You've always said St Ives stinks!' And how often he'd said it! she thought, unhappily. He had never shared her love for the small fishing village where they had played as children—gone to school.

'I don't have to eat the bloody things, do I?' he scoffed, an avid glimmer in his eyes. No doubt from the thought of all the money he could make, Fleur guessed, and was suddenly grateful that her aunt hadn't lived to suffer the painful knowledge of her son's deceitfulness.

Once or twice during the next couple of days she

considered asking him how he had acquired that secret
password, Phoenix—whether it had been from something he had heard, the careless misplacement of a file,
perhaps—but she thought better of it. It wasn't really
very important any more. But the brother/sister relationship they had enjoyed as children and which had been
deteriorating for years through having nothing in
common, now seemed totally lost—irretrievable—and a
mixture of sadness, pity and disgust were the only
emotions she could manage towards her cousin. She
couldn't even summon up any degree of bitterness over
the way he had abandoned her and, feeling awkward
sharing the same roof with him, she decided to leave on
the Monday morning. After all, there was no point in
burying herself down there when she had a job to look
for, she told herself, because even if she did go abroad
eventually, she had to live in the meantime.

'I'm sorry you felt you had to give up your job.' There
was the merest hint of contrition in David's apology as he
watched her climb into the taxi. 'Look . . . do you need
any money?' He produced a wad of notes, thrusting a few
in front of her as if that could solve everything. And as
though they were contaminated, Fleur recoiled from
them, shaking her head, embarrassed because the cab-
driver was watching without any reservations.

'Thanks . . . but I do have some savings,' she said
quietly, glad to be able to admit to a small measure of
independence.

David shrugged, closing the car door, stooping to rest
his elbows on the open window. 'Remember . . . I leave
on the twenty-ninth . . . but don't come and see me off.' A
hand lifted, silencing her immediate protest. 'I'd rather
you didn't. And I'm turning my half-share of the cottage
over to you.'

'Why?' she breathed, flabbergasted, because Aunt
Aggie had left them the house for their joint use. 'You'll

need a home in England when you want to come back.'

'Sorry, kid,' he said, through the sudden shrieking of seagulls, 'but I shan't be coming back.'

There was a note of positive finality in his voice and Fleur stared at him, at his familiar features, at the beginnings of a wispy, blond beard, desperately digesting every last detail of his slim frame through two hot pools which were suddenly blurring her vision. He was her only relative—however rotten or deceitful he had been. She didn't think she could bear not seeing him again.

Too choked to speak, she heard him issue a swift instruction to the driver, so that the car pulled away, and when she looked back, tears streaming down her cheeks, both her cousin and the cottage were out of sight.

'You had a visitor . . . on Saturday.' The landlady's gaze swivelled curiously to the open bedroom door and Fleur's suitcase lying in full view on the bed. 'I told him I thought you'd gone away for the weekend so he's coming back tonight.'

'Him?' Fleur's lungs could barely exhale the word as her pulse started racing. 'Did he say what time he'd be coming?'

'About eight, I think he said. Nice car, too.' A greying head nodded appreciatively. 'He left you these.'

Tremulously, Fleur stared at the bunch of red carnations as the landlady went back downstairs. Why would Elliot call . . . bring her flowers? she wondered, colour tinging the smooth skin over the high cheekbones. Did he really care about her as a person after all? Was he hoping to continue their relationship . . . ?

Through her haze of euphoria she felt a small cloud drift across her sunny horizon and burst, dampening the warm glow inside of her. They hadn't had a relationship. It had been a purely physical thing and she had been no more to him than a young, reasonably attractive woman

who had responded to his lovemaking. So was that the
sort of relationship he intended to continue with her?
Was that why he had been so keen to see her leave the
firm so that he could enjoy a solely physical affair with
her away from the curious glances and gossip at the
office?

No! her mind rebelled. She wasn't just another female
body to sate his desires. She wanted ... She cut her
thoughts dead, not daring to admit, even to herself, what
she really wanted. But nevertheless, despite her wariness
of his intentions, and continual warnings from her inner
self to play it cool when he arrived, she couldn't control
the sudden leap of her heart when the doorbell rang at
eight o'clock sharp, or the raging joy which pumped life
into her every pore as she flung open the front door.

CHAPTER EIGHT

FLEUR'S heart plummeted, the sight of the unexpected visitor rendering her speechless.

'The party,' he said, thinking she needed reminding. 'Chris Caldridge . . . remember?'

How could she forget? 'Of course.' Her smile hid an agony of disappointment. 'I was just a bit surprised . . .'

'You got my message . . . the flowers?' He looked perplexed. As perplexed as she was hurting inside.

'They were from you?' she mumbled, dumbly.

'I hope you didn't mind . . .'

Now he was being apologetic, and she couldn't just let him stand there and cry out that she did mind—very much! That he'd raised her hopes with his message and his flowers and dashed them to smithereens as soon as he'd knocked on her door, because that would have been rude, as well as cruel, and she couldn't be either. Besides, he looked friendly and cheerful, and she needed all the cheering up she could get at that moment, so that when he suggested going out to dinner, she accepted, gratefully.

'How did you find me?' she asked him in the small, intimate restaurant. She couldn't remember supplying him with her address. But then, she couldn't remember much of what she had said to him at that party, she thought, cringing as she considered the state she had been in.

'Gaby Asquith . . . I'm her next-door neighbour, remember?'

She did, and that he'd said he was a solicitor, although she hadn't really been listening to him that night. She'd been nursing some sick emotion watching Elliot with Gabrielle . . . until he'd come over and pulled her off that chair . . .

Remembering evoked a longing in her which she didn't want to acknowledge, so she turned her attention back to her companion as he went on, 'She was very co-operative in helping me track you down. I rang Steadman's to start with but they said you'd left, so I got Gaby to wheedle your surname and the locality where you lived out of that fiancé of hers. The rest was easy. I just looked you up in the telephone directory.'

Suddenly her beef stroganoff tasted like sawdust. 'Her . . . fiancé?' Fleur ventured, tentatively.

Chris wiped his mouth with a napkin, finishing his gammon. 'All except for the ring . . . so I'm led to understand. You know . . . you look lovely.'

His tawny eyes were appreciating the gold top-knot with the soft tendrils teased around the small oval face, the deeply shaded brown eyes and the full, creamy softness of her lips—glossed to match the bronze silk of her dress. He must have thought she'd gone to a great deal of trouble for him, she ruminated, battling against an urge to cry all over her noodles. And Gabrielle Asquith had helped him find her! But then the other woman had only had her own interests at heart. She must have thought her, Fleur, a positive threat at that party, she decided, achingly.

'You intended to get me tipsy that night, didn't you?' she accused softly, finishing her wine as dessert arrived.

'Not at all,' Chris defended, tucking into a huge piece of gâteau, making Fleur decide that he must have a weakness for rich cakes. That's how she remembered seeing him first—with a plate of gooey sponge. 'You looked unhappy . . . and I hoped that if you relaxed a bit you might start to enjoy yourself. I didn't know it would have that effect on you.'

'What effect?' she queried, hastily, colouring from the sudden embarrassing suspicion that she had done something outrageous she didn't yet know about.

'Only that you were blabbing on about someone locking you up,' he grinned, and with a sigh, Fleur relaxed.

'Was I?' she smiled innocently—hurting inside—and was reassured to see from the wry twist to his mouth that he hadn't believed a word of it.

The evening was agreeable enough—Chris's company pleasant. And when he bent to kiss her in the car outside her flat, suddenly she decided she wanted him to. Wanted him to show her that another man's touch could be as stimulating—as earth-shaking!—as Elliot's. But Chris's tentative kiss left her cold, and she pulled away from him, craving those lips which had bruised hers with their punishing kisses—that had made her sob with desire . . .

'I'll call you,' said Chris, unperturbedly, before driving away.

He kept his word, telephoning often, even persuading Fleur to see him again once or twice. But she didn't want to get involved, and told him so, having definitely decided that in the New Year she would be letting her cottage and going abroad.

Consequently, she was travelling down to Cornwall each weekend to decorate the little house—during the week accepting any temporary work the secretarial agency offered her. She should have stayed at Steadman's, she realised, with the benefit of hindsight—at least until she went away—because agency work didn't pay so well and it seemed pointless considering another permanent position now. True, she'd felt she couldn't face Elliot any longer, sensing his obvious contempt for her, but if she had been hoping that leaving the company would restore her sleep—her appetite—make her forget him, it hadn't. She still wasn't eating or sleeping properly—nor could she get her old boss out of her mind. She couldn't cross the street without seeing someone who resembled him, until they turned and she saw that they didn't have that same strength of character or that strong, thrusting jaw; couldn't hear the growl of a passing sportscar without looking up expectantly, hoping to see his. He was in her dreams, too, so that often she would wake in the dead of night, needing him, feverish for his kisses—the hard dominance of his body. And she would lie there for hours afterwards, tossing and turning, trying to make some sense of this complex and very agonising emotion. Until suddenly one night she understood. She loved Elliot Steadman!—the truth of it hitting her as hard as if she had been punched. No one could know so much wanting—so much need of another—without being irrevocably—irretrievably—in love. But how could she feel so deeply about someone who had kept her locked up for three days—who had despised and then humiliated her? she thought, tormentedly. It was crazy. Especially when he belonged to someone else.

But even that torturous admission didn't stop her telephoning Trudy the next day, desperate for any news she could get of him. At least Trudy would be able to tell her how he was.

'Moody,' the redhead announced in response to Fleur's casually delivered query. 'I know they say the position of command is a lonely one . . . but he doesn't seem to want to circulate amongst us mere menials as much as he used to. I think he's got a lot on his mind.'

'Like marriage?' Fleur nearly asked spontaneously— gripping the receiver hard—but stopped herself in time. She didn't want to know the answer to that.

'By the way,' Trudy's voice came buoyantly down the line, 'Stacey's leaving on Friday.' Effervescently, she plunged into a lengthy account of where the other girl was going, what the new computer programmer was like and Andrew Moreton's latest, unsuccessful attempt to stop smoking.

Of course. Elliot frowned upon the habit in the office, Fleur remembered, sharing his aversion to working in a smoke-filled atmosphere. But it looked as if he was going to have to suffer Andrew.

'Look . . . a few of us are having farewell drinks with Stacey in the pub Friday lunchtime,' Trudy was saying. 'Why don't you come?'

And risk seeing Elliot? Immediately, Fleur shunned the idea, her fingers twisting agitatedly in the loose platinum hair, but the voice at the other end of the line wasn't accepting any excuses.

'It will only be a few of us girls . . . so you won't be likely to bump into any of the management . . . although I don't know why you felt you had to leave at all just because your cousin had a row with the Board.' Guiltily, Fleur was reminded of the feeble explanation she had offered Trudy and the others girls for leaving Stead-man's. 'Elliot might be moody . . . but he's a pretty fair boss and I'm sure he wouldn't have held anything against *you*. You will come, won't you?'

Trudy's voice implored, and Fleur hesitated. What was the point in refusing anyway? She'd like to see her

old colleagues again. And as Trudy had pointed out,
there wouldn't be any likelihood of meeting any of the
senior management . . .

'All right,' she accepted, before she had realised it.

The rest of the week passed uneventfully. David left for
Australia with only a brief note of farewell which left
Fleur feeling so desolate that she was actually glad when
Friday came.

'You look stunning!' 'Trudy enthused in the pub that
lunchtime. 'Like something out of *Vogue*!' Enviously, she
was appreciating the grey, pin-striped suit Fleur had
teamed with a red silk blouse and red shoes—noting the
red moons against her earlobes, enhancing the sophisti-
cation of the blonde chignon. 'That's the advantage of
having a figure like a willow!' The telephonist grimaced
at her own generous curves beneath a green, knitted
dress, and Fleur smiled.

'I think you'll find most men prefer something they
can cuddle,' she remarked warmly, taking her friend's
compliments like a tonic. Looking better meant feeling
better, she had attempted to convince herself that
morning—taking care with her make-up, too, having not
bothered much with her appearance of late—and now
sitting amongst the small, animated group from her old
office, she had to admit that it did.

'. . . and apparently Frank Steadman was trying to
secure the right terms on that contract for months,' she
heard Stacey saying, guessing that she was talking about
Phoenix. 'And as soon as Elliot takes over . . . wham!
Prosperity reigns!'

'Wasn't he responsible for turning the S.A. subsidiary
into a gold mine?' Trudy asked, sipping a martini.

'And how!' someone else rejoined swiftly. 'Steadman
(Johannesburg) was in danger of being closed before he

stepped in with his marketing genius and within a year
he not only had it back on its feet . . . but taking record
profits! The man's unbelievable!'

Their avid remarks were whipping around Fleur like
wild flames—searing, hurting, consuming her. She
shouldn't have come, she thought, despairingly. She
should have known the new chairman would be
discussed. Since taking over the London company he had
set Steadman shares on an upward trend, and since the
finalising of the Phoenix deal they had reached a record
high. She read daily of his continuing success—she just
had to pick up a newspaper to find his name among
Britain's kings of industry—although at least there she
could pretend indifference to it. But here, where his
name was being mentioned continually by the people
with whom he worked—perhaps had spoken to that
morning—his influence was too strong to be ignored. A
little twist of pain threaded through her, making her
shiver, so that it was some moments before she realised
that the others were discussing Christmas. She breathed
a sigh of relief. At least that was a safe topic—unable to
cause her any distress, she thought, numbly, glancing
around at the bar's festive decorations and coloured
lights. And suddenly her blood seemed to run cold.

Glass poised at her lips, she couldn't take her gaze
away from the tall, dark figure who was shouldering his
way through the crowded bar. Glass in hand, he paused
to throw a comment at Andrew Moreton just behind him,
and panicky, Fleur's only thought was to get away before
Elliot saw her. But it was already too late.

'So this is where the female contingent of my staff
hangs out at lunchtime!'

He was standing above them, the hard, commanding

mouth curved in a smile, his eyes, Fleur realised, with a
stab of pain, noting her presence in the little group
without a flicker of emotion.

'Would you mind rephrasing that please, Elliot!'
Stacey laughed, as he put his glass down on their table.

It looked like neat Scotch, Fleur thought, staring at the
amber liquid—not trusting her eyes to look anywhere
else. She could sense the ripple of excitement his
presence was causing among the other girls, and in
herself she could feel a warm flush spreading from her
toes up.

'Gosh . . . I'm sorry,' she heard Trudy whisper to her.
'He usually goes to The Crown.'

But he was asking them what they wanted to drink
and, heart pounding against her rib-cage, Fleur tensed,
unbelievably tongue-tied as he spoke to her—as her
trembling gaze met and locked with his. She saw the hint
of a mocking smile flit across his lips, and then he was
suggesting softly—helping her—'Medium dry white?'

'T-thanks.' It came out as an embarrassed stammer,
and she was glad when he and Andrew pushed their way
back to the bar.

'How did he know you only drank white wine?'
Trudy's surprised voice sounded muffled—far away. 'He
could see you were drinking tomato juice last time . . .'

'And did you notice the way he was looking at her,
Trudy? Like he wanted to get inside that blouse!'

'My goodness! She's blushing!'

They were teasing her—she knew that—but it was
disconcerting enough that Elliot had come to their table
in the first place, without having to put up with their
comments as well, she thought, dizzily. Trudy, though,
was making much more of it than the others.

'You weren't by any chance seeing him socially, were
you?' Above the hubbub of idle conversation and the
clatter of plates and cutlery, the telephonist's whisper

was one of incredulity—sudden awareness. 'Was that why you felt you had to leave so quickly? Did something go wrong?'

'Please Trudy ... not now,' Fleur appealed, shakily. And realised, too late, that that agonised petition was all the redhead had needed to confirm her suspicions.

Through a burst of ebullient laughter from across the room, Fleur heard her breathe—her voice a combination of astonishment and envy, 'Were you sleeping with him?'

She shot her friend such a silencing look that Trudy backed down, but there was an excited flush to the full cheeks, and Fleur sighed in despair. Trudy was nice, but she would have a field day in the office with something like this. And it was too late now to try and bluff her way out of it.

The men were back, and with a thudding heart Fleur saw Elliot choose the stool immediately opposite her own. It was a deliberate move, she decided, her head in a spin, because there were other empty seats around the table, and intuition told her that he had sat there solely to assess her reaction.

Well, she'd show him that he couldn't affect her in the slightest! she resolved, trying to feign indifference to him as she sipped the wine he had brought her, but it was difficult when that strong, dark magnetism was unsettling her so much. Even though he was engaged in conversation with Stacey, she could feel his eyes upon her—cool and reflective—never leaving her for a moment, and hopelessly her hand was starting to tremble.

'What are you doing now, Fleur?'

He was speaking to *her*? Unprepared, she couldn't answer for a moment, and was relieved when Trudy intervened effusively with, 'She's modelling! Can't you tell?'

It was the perfect cue for him to make an unashamed

study of her figure and he did, his gaze intent—
undressing her—as it ran over her soft curves, so that she
couldn't keep from blushing. He smiled absently—aware
of her discomfiture—but there was a thin crease between
his eyebrows.

'Seriously,' he said, his voice soft, and for a moment it
was as if they were alone in a small bubble of intimacy. 'I
thought you were going abroad. Where are you working
at the moment?'

Fleur swallowed, sensing Trudy's keen interest in what
they were saying. She was obviously eager to pick up
anything which might suggest that she and Elliot had
been lovers, Fleur thought, on tenterhooks in case her
friend said something embarrassing, and beneath the
elegant, grey suit she could feel herself breaking out into
a sweat.

'Oh ... here and there,' she murmured casually,
surprising even herself with her coolness, although she
didn't trust her voice to explain her future plans.

The crease in Elliot's forehead deepened. 'You mean
you're temping?'

She nodded, flicking her tongue over suddenly dry lips.
Why had he managed to make it sound so discrediting?

'That can't be very satisfying ... offering your services
to anyone.'

His deprecating tone incensed her. She knew she had
been impetuous throwing up her job as she had. But
wasn't it his fault that she'd been forced into this position
in the first place? she thought, fuming.

Quickly draining her glass, she got to her feet and
heard Andrew's voice drift towards her with a cloud of
blue smoke. 'What's all this I hear about you modelling,
Fleur?'

She forced herself to smile, telling him it was only a
joke. He was a wizard in the office—superbly efficient—
she remembered, there being no one better to serve as

Elliot's right-hand man. But his brilliance made him vague—like an absent-minded professor—and as usual, she decided, unduly irritated, he'd only listened to half the conversation and got it all wrong.

'I must go.'

She was glad when she was outside, heading for the bus stop, her legs still weak from meeting Elliot. What influence did the man have over her to make her feel like this? she wondered, desperately. He had only to speak a few words to her to turn her into a trembling, mindless wreck. And the humiliating thing was he knew how he affected her, she thought, shuddering, deciding that the best thing she could do in future would be to keep as far away from him as she could possibly get. And that ruled out any more lunchtime drinks in The Duke!

She stepped into the road—hectic with lunch-hour traffic—dodging cars in a hazardous attempt to reach the bus stop. A horn blared, startling her, and she froze, seeing the blue saloon heading straight for her. She was going to be killed! she thought, riveted. And gasped as a strong arm caught her elbow, steering her out of harm's way.

'What the hell are you trying to do ... get yourself knocked down?'

Elliot's words were a hard reprimand as he assisted her safely on to the pavement, but Fleur pulled away from him, her eyes overbright, cheeks flushed.

'You followed me!' she accused, heart hammering out of control.

'My God! You always were astute.'

'Why?' she breathed, vehemently, wishing he'd go away. She could feel her whole body weakening, her legs threatening to buckle under her.

'Astute parents? I don't know.'

'You know what I meant!' she exhaled, hating him for his flippant remarks. Couldn't he see he was breaking her heart just being there?

'I think we should talk,' he said, suddenly serious, and reached to ease her gently out of someone's path. The simple gesture brought her closer to him, and she could smell the tantalising spice of his aftershave lotion.

'What about?' she whispered, tremulously, fighting an unbearable longing to be in his arms.

'Look . . .' Elliot shot a glance round at the bus-queue—the roaring traffic—and ran impatient fingers through his hair. 'Could we go somewhere a little more private? I'll give you a lift.'

'No!' She said it too quickly—too meaningfully—and saw one thick eyebrow lift in cognizance. He knew exactly why she had refused him, but she didn't care. She didn't want to be alone with him. Risk her emotions. Risk him seeing them. She couldn't face the ultimate humiliation of that.

'What are you doing tonight?'

His softly spoken question made her heart leap. 'Why?' she asked, slightly breathless from its sudden, wild pounding. Was he asking her out?

'Don't you ever answer a question without a question?' he threw at her, half-annoyed. 'I want to see you, isn't that enough?'

She turned the pale gold of her head to look at him, the tiny amber flecks in her eyes mirroring disbelief. A cold gust of wind cut through her open trench coat, penetrating the light suit, and she shivered.

'You've lost weight.'

Elliot's intense examination of her made her colour rise, yet in the hard, angular lines of his face she thought she read concern. Did he care? A ray of hope burst through the clouds of her misery, warming her despite the December day. Did he care even a little?

'Have dinner with me,' he persisted, his voice low—personal. 'Then we can talk in more relaxed surroundings.'

Fleur studied him obliquely. 'About what?' she managed to enquire in a cool voice this time, though she was fighting an overwhelming impulse to accept. A bus had pulled up alongside the kerb, and the queue was starting to board it, one or two curious pairs of eyes turning their way.

'For God's sake!' Exasperated, Elliot urged her back against the building behind them and the modest amount of privacy it offered, looking almost in pain as he breathed, raggedly, 'We shared some rather intimate moments . . . remember?'

Did she! The brand of his lovemaking would be stamped on her for the rest of her days! But it was he who hadn't wanted to remember . . .

'Don't remind me,' she said bitterly, and would have moved towards the bus if he hadn't stopped her.

'Still trying to deny what you felt?' His jaw had tightened in anger, but his voice was thick with some other emotion as he said, 'There's still ill-feeling between us and I think we should have an end to it . . . clear up this pointless animosity . . .'

'And then?' she queried, mindlessly, her reasoning clouded by his nearness.

Broad shoulders lifted in a shrug. 'That depends.'

'On what?' She hardly dared breathe now.

'You . . . me,' he said, softly. His eyes were dark with emotion and she felt as if she were drowning in them, floundering blissfully in a high, warm sea. Had what she heard about him and Gabrielle been speculative rumour? Exaggerated gossip? Wasn't he getting engaged to her after all. 'Fleur . . .'.

His voice caressed as he drew her closer to him, and his fingers on her wrist were stimulating and warm. A few feet away the last person was stepping on to the bus, but she didn't notice, the sexual pull between her and Elliot so great that all she could think of—wanted!—was for him to take her away somewhere secluded and make love to her.

'We must talk,' he reiterated, his voice quietly urgent. 'Tonight.' He dropped a swift glance towards his watch. 'As much as I'd love to, I can't make it before. I'm seeing Gaby at two.'

Damn him! It was like being plunged into cold water and wounded she tore herself away from him, tears blinding her, a pain like a knife twisting round and round somewhere under her ribs. Damn him!

'There's nothing to say,' somehow she managed to get out in a small, strangled voice, and she was runing for the bus, jumping on without a glance back, numb with pain and bitter disappointment as the vehicle bore her away.

She hadn't told anyone she was giving up the flat. Only Chris Caldridge, and only then because he had called round while she was packing the last of her belongings.

'I need to spend more time at the cottage to get it into some sort of order before I let it,' she remembered telling him, although she hadn't informed him of what had prompted this very sudden decision. The truth was that after meeting Elliot in the pub on Friday she had had to get away—and what better time than at the first available weekend? Seeing him again had proved only one thing—he didn't care about her in the slightest. And while she felt she couldn't face ever meeting him by chance like that again, she knew there was every likelihood of it as long as she stayed in London. He might even have called! And she knew that once alone with him, she would have been in complete danger of revealing just how much he meant to her.

That he wanted *her* was without dispute. She had

sensed it in every tense muscle of his body—read the
wanting in his eyes as surely as if he had declared it—and
it had been such an intensity of emotion that for a few
moments at that bus stop she had been fooled into
thinking he cared. Well he didn't, she thought, numbly,
staring out at the rugged Cornish coast, and she'd been
utterly stupid and naïve to imagine for one moment that
he did. She was nothing more to him than a sexual
diversion until he married Gabrielle, she realised, her
breath catching painfully in her chest. And when he did,
she didn't want to be around to know about it.

Hard work, she found, was an antidote to pain, and
during the next few weeks there was plenty of that. Long,
lonely days when she would try to drive away the agony
of longing inside her—spring-cleaning, wall-papering
and painting—only to feel it surface with crushing
intensity during the longer, lonelier nights.

I'm going crazy, she thought, worriedly, after one
particularly bad night, and coming downstairs, found a
letter from Trudy. It thanked Fleur for a book she'd
recently returned, but her stomach churned queasily
when she noticed it made some reference to Elliot.

'He's as moody as ever,' the redhead had written.

'Perhaps the future's weighing heavily on him . . .
although that doesn't sound like our indomitable
leader! Still it's *his* decision . . . I expect you've read
about it . . . but none of us here thought he'd take the
big step so soon. Apparently he's staying with the
Asquiths this weekend to finalise arrangements . . .
so it's all on for next month!'

There was more general news, but Fleur couldn't read it,
an intolerable depth of anguish seeming to twist her
insides. So Elliot's marriage plans had even been
published in the newspapers—that's how certain they
were, she realised, such a wave of desolation washing

over her she felt as if she were drowning.

She had to get out. She took a long walk over the cliffs, trying to ease the anguish in a vain attempt at convincing herself she despised Elliot Steadman. After all, if it hadn't been for him she wouldn't be suffering now, she told herself irrationally: the loss of her self-respect, her job and her flat; this unbelievable pain. But resentment sprang—like her tears—from a well of bitter jealousy, fed by a love which was whole and complete—even if it was tearing her apart—and she knew she could no more deny that love than she could tell her lungs to stop drawing breath. He was in her blood, and despairingly she wondered whether she would ever be able to love anyone else again.

But it was her own naïvety in trusting David that had led to Elliot abducting her—ultimately she accepted that; he'd been no less a victim of her cousin's deceit than she had. And it was no one's fault but her own if she'd fallen in love with her gaoler when he'd obviously felt nothing for her but contempt. The only redeeming factor, she realised, with torturous gratitude, was that he would never know.

Needing something to do to stop herself thinking about him, she returned to the cottage and began clearing out David's old room ready for decorating. She was still working, long after dusk, and it was while she was sorting through a cupboard that she came across the papers. Plans, specifications and information sheets regarding a scheme Steadman's had been proposing.

Icy fingers clutched her heart. Was this yet another of the firm's projects her cousin had turned to his own ends?

With trembling hands she studied the papers. They were dated about eighteen months previously. Not wanting to be involved—to face anything else David might have done wrong—her first thought was to throw them out, but she hesitated, knowing that that wasn't the right thing to do. The right thing would be to send them to Elliot—or at the very least, to ring him and ask his advice on what she should do with them, she thought, uneasily. But that meant contacting him—something she didn't have the slightest inclination to do. Perhaps if she sent the documents with a brief note but no return address, then she wouldn't need to get involved with him personally, she deliberated. But dismissed that idea, deciding that, painful though it might be, she had to know as soon as possible how important those papers were—and what David had been doing with them.

But there was no telephone at the cottage, so first thing the following morning she trudged to the nearest kiosk, fighting such a barrage of emotions when she heard Elliot's voice on the line, that it was difficult keeping her own steady as she told him about her find.

'No, don't send them,' he counselled, when she put the suggestion to him. 'It may be possible to destroy them, but we'll have to make sure.' Adding, to her utter horror, 'I've a meeting in Exeter on Friday afternoon . . . I'll pop down afterwards and take a look at them.'

'No!' Fleur protested in sudden panic. The last thing she wanted was for him to come down there. But his insistence quashed any argument against it and, defeatedly, she made her way back home with tears of frustration burning her eyes.

She didn't want to see him again. And in a deep agony of emotion knew she was so opposed to it because, contrarily, she wanted it too much. Oh how she wanted it! But she'd spent the last few weeks trying to repair the damage he'd caused to her heart and her pride, and their was no way that she was going to let him affect her in the same way a second time.

Why couldn't he have left her alone?

The plaintive crying of gulls seemed to echo her misery from the humiliation she'd suffered, the inconvenience, the pain. And suddenly her need of her aunt was so great that as she let herself into the house she could almost smell the warm cloves in Agnes Markham's fruit pies— almost expected her to come bustling out of the kitchen, ready to listen, to console and advise. But of course it was only her imagination, Fleur accepted, an ache of loss so painful in her chest she had to catch her breath, although she was struggling to understand the jumble of words which had sprung from nowhere to her mind.

'Take life with both hands and twist it the way you want it to go ... otherwise it will twist you.' That old adage she had heard over and over as a child came back to her as vividly now as if her aunt had just spoken it—a little woman with courage who had worked hard to bring up two children on her own.

And suddenly self-pity was dissipating on a wave of hot anger. It was as if the floodgates of a dam had burst open, letting out all the depression and negative emotions she had been nurturing for weeks. New spirit poured into her with a surge of fresh energy and determination, and she blinked back her tears, ramming her hands hard into the back pockets of her jeans.

She was her aunt's niece, wasn't she? With her aunt's courage—her strength for survival? So what was she doing, thinking of running away? She didn't want to go abroad, so she wouldn't. She'd go back to London. Find another job in computers, and a new flat, too—one even better than before. But prior to that ... she was going to have to face Elliot, and that wasn't going to be easy after the way he had treated her.

She could excuse the way he had acted initially—the heat of his rage when he'd thought her a thief. After all, he'd not only had his company's interests at heart and those of his staff, but also a duty to a father he'd loved. She could understand his motives—why he'd despised her so much. But while she'd been his prisoner, why had he seemed so bent on wringing a sexual response from her? she thought bitterly, her pride smarting from the memory of how readily she had shown him that response. Had it been simply lust on his part? Opportunism, finding a reasonably attractive girl under his control? She didn't think so. More probably it had been purely cynical exploitation of her because of what he believed her to be, she thought, shuddering, although, if that were the case, what explanation was there for his behaviour at the party?

She moved over to the window, opening it to breathe the cold, revitalising air.

By then he'd known that she wasn't the fraudulent creature he'd suspected her of being—he'd even shown snatches of tenderness towards her that night. But he had still wanted her surrender—the ultimate domination of her—even if he hadn't made use of his subsequent victory, so perhaps it had been his intention all along to have her capitulation and then reject her. But for what reason? she asked herself, piqued. To punish her? Masculine ego? She wasn't sure. But whatever it was, she thought angrily, he had humiliated her beyond belief. How would he have felt being placed in such a vulnerable position?

She bit her lip as an idea suddenly occurred to her. If Elliot Steadman was so determined to come here, why shouldn't she take advantage of the fact? She knew it would be a risk to her emotions seeing him again, but he wasn't her boss any more—he didn't have any control over her life. And perhaps the one way she could shatter the idea that he had—that she'd never be able to escape his influence—would be to pay him back in his own coin!

He was just going to 'pop in' was he? Well, that's what *he* thought, she decided, resolutely, tugging off her headscarf to free the wild, platinum silk. He was going to spend more than a few hours in Cornwall, although he didn't know it yet. But when he arrived on Friday . . .

She put her hands to her cheeks. Felt them burning—
burning from a peculiar excitement. She'd trap him!
That's what she'd do. She'd give him a taste of his own
medicine. Let *him* see what it was like to be inconven-
ienced for a while—held somewhere against his will.
Thunderously, her heart pounded a warning at her
reckless decision, but her eyes were sparkling from the
wild prospect of doing to him exactly what he had done
to her.

She'd trap him! Just as he'd trapped her when he had
taken her to the mews. And she knew just how she was
going to do it!

CHAPTER NINE

PUTTING the finishing touches to her make-up, Fleur started as the doorbell suddenly chimed. Elliot was earlier than she'd expected!

She cast a cursory glance at her reflection. Dark eyes accentuated by a subtle, tawny shadow, their thick, feathery lashes lengthened by mascara. A hint of blusher adding necessary colour to her pallid cheeks and a soft cream emphasising the generous curve of her mouth. The effect was good, one which, with the loose blonde tendrils falling from the casually swept-up hair, allowed her the natural look she had taken such great pains to achieve. After all, she didn't want Elliot thinking she had gone to any great lengths for him!

'You *were* expecting me,' he drawled with some amusement when he saw her astonished face so that quickly she murmured an affirmative response. What she hadn't expected was that he would be wearing a beautiful silver-grey suit and snowy shirt, and his immaculate appearance only served to emphasise the recklessness of her plan. 'May I come in?'

He shouldn't have needed to ask! Nervously she cleared her throat to utter, 'Of course,' silently chiding herself for letting him unsettle her. If this was how she intended to carry on she could kiss goodbye to her little scheme right now.

'You've lost more weight.' In the tiny living-room, Elliot's swift glance had taken in the cheerful fire, the dresser with its antique china and the two fireside chairs, but his grey gaze had come to rest on Fleur, his slow, cool appraisal of her figure beneath the crimson velour

leisure-suit bringing natural colour to her cheeks. 'Have
you been unwell?'

She saw the thin line between his dark eyebrows, but
shook her head, her heartbeat unrhythmic, every nerve
tingling into life at the sight and sound and scent of him.
Trust him to notice!

'What Trudy said in The Duke that day set me
thinking . . . I might just become a model,' she bluffed
with feigned flippancy. 'A minimal covering of skin is
one of the prim requisites so I understand.' That sounded
better than, 'Yes . . . I've been pining for you.'

'I don't believe you.' His words were slow—censuring,
his eyes too probing—too intent—beneath the sharply
defined brows. 'Lose any more and all you'll be modelling
is a white shroud and a harp.'

Flattering! she thought, her attention drawn to the
long, tanned fingers slipping the car keys into his trouser
pocket. Her eyes registered the movement with calculat-
ing awareness—noted the narrowness of his hips beneath
the grey cloth, the muscular strength of his thighs—and
her mouth went dry just thinking about the havoc she
intended to wreak upon him.

'What's really the trouble?'

'What?' She shot him an almost guilty look and said
quickly, 'Nothing . . . nothing at all.' Her smile trembled.
'Sit down and I'll get those papers.'

When she brought them back from the dresser, he was
lounging in one of the chairs, his long legs stretched out
before him, crossed at the ankle, and the light from the
fire was lending an almost demonic look to his dark
features. She must be crazy, she thought, thinking that a
plan to trap him could work! When he had been three
hundred miles away it had seemed easy, but she'd
forgotten how commanding he was—how utterly masculine and strong. Even sitting down he dominated the
whole room!

'You seem ... unnaturally agitated.' He took the documents from her shaky hand, his eyes following the soft line of her body beneath the crimson velour. 'What's the matter?'

'Nothing,' she lied, and grabbed the decanter on the dresser for a diversion. Nothing except for the fact that her whole, carefully devised plan was in danger of crumbling! 'Scotch?'

When he took the glass she handed him—his head still bowed in concentration—she had to clench her fingers to restrain the sudden urge to run them through that thick crop of dark hair. The desire, she realised shamefully, was even stronger than her fear that those papers were stolen, and she said rather breathlessly, before courage failed her, 'I haven't eaten yet. I thought that as you'd be coming straight from a meeting you'd want dinner ... so I put a casserole in the oven.'

The smile he flashed her was so suggestive that a blaze of embarrassed colour suffused her cheeks. What was wrong with her? She had to keep her cool. Keep that clever brain of his from guessing that she was plotting something horrendous. And beef casserole was all part of the plan.

'Then why are we bothering with these?'

She watched in amazement as he tore up the designs, notes and specifications—most of which he'd barely scanned—and tossed them on to the fire. Weren't they as important as she'd thought?

'No ... they weren't stolen,' he said, answering her silently conveyed question, and he got to his feet, his impressive stature making her step back instinctively. 'Harlem was a project David was working on personally for me, but it was aborted more than fifteen months ago. I knew he brought work away some weekends. Those papers have probably been here since the scheme fell through.'

'Then there's nothing to worry . . .' She broke off, the
relief in her eyes—illuminated by the sudden burst of
flames in the grate—quickly changing to angry fire. 'I
told you what those papers referred to on the phone . . .
you could have told me all this then . . .'

'I could have . . . but I wanted to see you again.' The
hard mouth twitched at the corners as he made a move
towards her. 'As much I think . . . as you wanted to see
me.'

'No,' Fleur denied hotly, backing away, desperate to
convince him—keep him from touching her.

'Isn't that the reason you telephoned instead of putting
them in the post to me? You could have you know . . .
without bothering to contact me at all. What other reson
could there be?'

She wanted to tell him—that it was because she had
had to know about David—but the words stuck in her
throat.

'I'm not the least bit interested in you, Elliot
Steadman,' she said, tremulously, instead. 'You've got it
all wrong.' And gasped when his hand shot out to restrain
her from moving away, the strong fingers closing with
startling tenacity around her wrist.

'No?' he queried, drawing her back to him, a sceptical
twist to his lips. 'When you've obviously spent hours
trying to look as though you haven't tried!'

Oh he was shrewd! Little waves of guilt were breaking
on the shores of her conscience, and she could feel small
beads of perspiration forming above her top lip. He was
far, far shrewder than she'd given him credit for! How
could her plan possibly work?

'Let go of me,' she tried saying firmly, but her voice
shook, and he was pulling her closer, one arm encircling
her waist, his head dipping to press warm lips against her
throat, making her stiffen with desire. The warm, hard
contact of his body and the fresh, clean smell of him were

stripping her of her defences—turning her legs to jelly—and in a blind panic she knew she had to stop him. If she succumbed now, he'd go away smug, thinking he was right—that all she had wanted was to see him again—and she couldn't let him think that, no matter how true it was. She'd rather go ahead with her plan. Suffer his anger—his rage even—when he found out he'd walked into a trap, rather than let him leave forever thinking her a love-sick fool.

'I'll get that casserole,' she murmured, tremblingly, tugging away from him.

'I thought you only drank white.' Elliot was scanning the heavy carafe Fleur brought to the table, brimming with a rich, ruby wine. It had to be red.

'White isn't the thing to have with beef,' she answered, her voice surprisingly steady. 'I'm trying to educate my taste buds.'

He looked amused, but she thought she had managed to convince him. After all, he wasn't to know that she hated it—wouldn't have dreamed of buying Beaujolais if she hadn't known he was coming.

Filling both glasses, she set the carafe purosefully on the dresser behind Elliot and sat down, her eyes uncertain as he sampled the casserole. It was made from her own recipe of mushrooms, tomatoes, courgettes and noodles. 'Do you like it?'

'It's delicious' Chewing he gave her a lazy smile. 'You'll make someone a good wife.'

It sounded exactly what it was—a casual remark—and it hurt.

'Thanks,' she attempted lightly in response, tucking into her own dinner.

'Like Chris Caldridge, for instance?'

She looked up. Saw that the smile had gone from Eliiott's face, and as his fingers closed around his glass, she noted the gesture with a nervous little shudder.

'Who told you about him?'

Elliot's mouth curled humourlessly. 'Word travels.'

Of course. Gabrielle. Hadn't she tried her utmost to bring the two of them together?

'Any objections?' she asked, acidly, deciding against telling him that she had only seen Chris once or twice. It was safer that way.

He shook his head, not in reply, she realised, but in disapproval. 'You could do better,' he said, gently.

'Oh?' An eyebrow raised curiously, Fleur watched as he took a good gulp of his wine, nervous tension mounting. She had to do it soon . . .

'You've got too much spirit for a man like that,' he enlarged, after a moment. 'You need someone more forceful. Someone who'll know how to bring out that passionate nature of yours . . . who'll know how to control it.'

'Like you?' she was taunting before she could stop herself, eyes sparking anger from the chauvinistic cheek of the man!

A broad shoulder lifted in a shrug, and contrary to all rational thought and judgement, Fleur's heart leaped. But hot colour stole across her pale skin as she said, scathingly, 'Are you suggesting we have an affair?'

Elliot's mouth compressed. 'Hardly.'

And the finality and dismissal in that one word was like a door being slammed in her face. He was marrying Gabrielle Asquith—how could she forget that? And she knew Elliot to be a man of too much principle to consider taking a mistress and a wife. That first night in the mews he had said he valued honesty and integrity—qualities she knew were firmly installed in his own character and which she had no doubt he would exercise in any marriage he entered into. No, he was only playing with *her*, she realised—testing her responses again as he'd done that day in The Duke.

Pain lined her face, and suddenly she felt sick. She didn't want him sitting there across the table from her. It didn't matter how much she craved to run her fingers along that dark jawline—touch that fascinating mole on his cheek, he could never belong to her. She wanted him to go. Yet she couldn't send him away thinking she'd just been chasing him—she couldn't bear the humiliation of that. She had to go ahead with her plan no matter what, And now, before she lost courage completely.

'Have some more wine.'

Jumping up, she reached for the carafe, ostensibly to refill his glass, but her hand was trembling so much that even without intent she would have been in danger of letting the vessel slip, as it did, catching Elliot's shoulder to send Beaujolais tumbling out all over the beautiful silver-grey suit.

'What . . .' He made some sound in his throat like a drowning man, his chair scraping the floor as he shot to his feet. Red wine was everywhere. Over the tablecloth. Over the rug. Over the curtains. But chiefly over him. He seemed to have taken most of it in his lap, but his jacket and previously snowy shirt were patterned with crimson spots. There was even a splash on his cheek.

'Oh Elliot . . . I'm sorry!' Fleur stood waving her hands helplessly in the air. 'I'm sorry . . . I really am!' If she had been trying for an Academy Award she knew she couldn't have feigned more sincerity and to add strength to her performance she darted out into the kitchen, rushing back with a damp cloth which she began wiping over the expensive suit. 'I'm sorry . . . really I am.'

'So you should be!' He spread his arms hopelessly, flicking red wine off the fingers of one hand, his mouth curling in discomfort. 'I'd better get out of these things.'

He glanced down at his trousers and Fleur paused from her mopping-up operation, considering the sorry state of

him. His shirt and jacket weren't too spoiled, but his
trousers were saturated, and she had the delightful
suspicion that the wine was seeping through to his
underpants.

'Look . . . why don't you step into the shower?' she
suggested, helpfully, rather too eagerly. 'This might be
the back of beyond but we do *have* a shower. Then you
can pass me out your clothes and I can wash the shirt and
then see what I can do with the suit.'

'You're too kind,' he drawled, sarcastically, giving her
a highly reproving look, 'but that won't be necessary. I'll
get it dried off tonight and have it professionally cleaned
when I get back to London.'

He was going to be awkward! She hadn't reckoned
on that.

'I insist,' she said resolutely, sticking out her chin and
hoping he'd concede. 'I caused all the trouble, so it's the
least I can do . . . although I'm afraid you'll have to drape
yourself in towels for a while. David didn't leave any
clothes behind and,' with a cursory glance over those
broad shoulders which caused a funny feeling in her
stomach, added, 'they wouldn't have fitted if he had.'

At last he gave in.

'I'll bring you those towels,' she said, directing him to
the bathroom, and coming back from the linen cupboard, realised that he hadn't wasted any time. His
clothes were discarded on the edge of the bath. Water
was already running in the shower—clouds of steam
issuing up from behind the curtain—and a stealthy
glance at the near-transparent plastic revealed the
outline of Elliot's totally naked body. Dropping the
towels as if they were hot coals, Fleur scooped up the
stained clothes and made a quick exit, the thought of so
little between her and that magnificent male physique
disconcerting beyond belief.

Were the keys to the Jaguar still in his pocket? At the

top of the stairs she stopped to make a swift check and
found that they were. Blood rushed to her temples,
making her breathless, her throat dry. Now she had him
exactly where she wanted him! And triumphantly
clutching every stitch he had been wearing, she raced
downstairs and out of the back door to put the final part
of her plan into action.

She was on her hands and knees, mopping up the last
of the Beaujolais when he came down, and the sight of
him sent the adrenalin pumping through her veins.

Barefoot, one white towel slung low over his hips, his
beautiful broad chest was exposed in all its glory, that
wiry tangle of dark hair stretching across it, tapering
down to a thin line to just below his navel—a striking
contrast against the still—deep tan of his skin. Another
towel was draped around his neck, and his thick, dark
hair was swept back—damp from the shower.

Fleur scrambled to her feet, her cheeks flushed from
the night air, but more from Elliot's totally unsettling
presence.

'Would you be a good girl and do me a small favour?'

She had been trying not to look at him, but now she
had no choice.

'What?' she queried, curious.

'There's a robe in the Jag. My keys . . .' His hand went
to his hip. 'They're in my suit,' he remembered. 'What
have you done with it?'

Big brown eyes lifted innocently to his. 'Your suit?'
Fleur echoed, dumbly, although there were butterflies
stirring uneasily in her stomach.

'Yes, my suit,' he reiterated, with just the smallest hint
of impatience. 'The one you so kindly offered to take and
clean up for me.'

'Oh that one!' She gave a knowing little laugh, but
deep down inside was beginning to wish that she hadn't
started this. She was playing a very dangerous game and

try though she did to ignore it, a small, inner voice was warning her that she could well end up the loser. 'I tried,' she prevaricated, careful to keep her voice under control, 'but it wouldn't come clean so I . . . threw it away.'

Dark brows met in questioning amazement. 'You *what*?'

She gave a careless shrug. 'I threw it away,' she repeated, only then considering what he had said about there being a robe in the car. Had he been planning to stay the night?

She watched him push open the door to the kitchen— glance around the other room. 'All right,' he accepted with a half-smile, shoulders dropping in a heavy sigh. 'Joke's over. Now where are my clothes?'

Fleur took a deep breath and steeled herself. He wasn't going to like this. 'You can't see because it's too dark . . . but there's a pile of rocks out there . . .' She indicated towards the window with the slightest movement of her head, 'about a mile out to sea. I should think your clothes could have just about reached it by now.'

'You're kidding?' The note of utter disbelief in Elliot's voice strongly suggested that he *was* beginning to believe her. 'What the hell possessed you to do that?' Strong features contorted, he was looking at her as though she were a complete imbecile, and nervously Fleur moved back, feeling the scarlet colour creeping up her throat. She was crazy even considering going on with this fiasco, she thought—hoping to do to him what he'd done to her. After all, when he'd held her at the mews, he had had that added weapon of brute strength on his side—even though he hadn't used it. And he still had the benefit of that weapon.

Suddenly, she didn't care any more. 'How does it feel, Elliot?' she challenged bitterly and she was trembling— her heart hammering like a drum-roll against her ribs. 'How does it feel being held somewhere against your

will? To know you can't leave no matter how much you
want to?'

Frustratingly, she was near to tears—had to struggle to
stop her composure sliding away from her altogether.

The broad shoulders sagged in comprehension. 'So
that's it,' he acknowledged, quietly, and she could have
died when she saw the deprecating curl of his lips. But
then what had she expected? A handshake? 'Is that what
you want?' he asked, heavily. 'Revenge?'

No, I want you! her mind screamed in agony, and she
had to turn away from him so that he wouldn't see the hot
tears which were stinging her eyelids. Revenge wasn't
sweet, whoever had said it was, she was suddenly
realising. It was childish. Childish and painful and very
degrading. She wished she hadn't plotted this whole
thing—had never even telephoned him in the first place.
But behind the excuses she had made to him—to
herself—had been an overwhelming compulsion to
contact him again, she had to admit that now.

'Isn't it only natural?' she queried, her back to him
still, desperate that he shouldn't guess the truth. 'After
the way you treated me ... humiliated me?' Her tears
seemed to be pressing down on her like an immense
weight, and she could hear her voice rising above it. 'You
lock me up! Treat me like a criminal! And after you'd got
me virtually begging you to take me to bed you ignored
me like ... like ...' She couldn't keep the sobs out of her
voice—hardly cared now because of the pain from
remembering his casual indifference to her in the office.
'Like it was some debt I owed you! You must have felt
good!' She swung back to him, eyes sparkling with
tears and hurt anger, a twist of pale gold tumbling down
on to crimson velour. 'It isn't very nice to be inconven-
ienced ... *caged up*, is it?' she threw at him poignantly,
adding for good measure, 'And there isn't a phone here

either because Aunt Aggie never bothered to have one put in!'

That sounded childish, too, she admitted silently, but she didn't care any longer what he thought of her—what he did. She looked down at her sandalled feet and noticed that they were splashed with Beaujolais. It was the same colour as her toenails, she thought, absently, and looking up again was suprised to see Elliot's mouth curving in a smile.

'You know ... there's more spirit in you than in a cellarful of Southern Comfort,' he remarked, fingers splayed on his hips. And she thought, this is all wrong. He should be livid. Not standing there damn well grinning!

'All right ... I concede ... I'm your prisoner.' He spread his hands—palms upwards—in defeat. 'Now what are you going to do with me?'

Fleur stared at him, twisting her hands, unable to comprehend his humour over the situation. She hadn't been prepared for that.

'I don't know,' she communicated to him somewhat bashfully, glancing down at her feet again.

'Might I make a suggestion?'

'What?' she asked defeatedly, looking at him.

He was crossing the space between them—ignoring the warning she flashed him—to pull her into his arms.

'May I suggest that the lady's all angry and twisted up inside because she's in love?'

'No!' Hands pushing against the bare chest, desperately Fleur tried to escape the iron vice of his hold, the feel of coarse hair beneath her fingers and the warmth of his near-naked body, making her senses spin. 'Let me go!'

'No.' His voice was firm as he drew her closer, pressing her soft body against the warm, hard angles of his. She gave a soft moan of protest, riveted by the sensations flooding through her, but Elliot's mouth was swooping to

RUDE AWAKENING 173

take hungry possession of hers. She tried to resist. Tried pushing him away and failed. And realised, in hazy panic, that however much her brain rebuffed him, her body was making positive demands of its own.

Desire erupted in her, flowing through her veins like molten lava on its course of destruction—golden and beautiful and devastating. A primeval instinct to surrender blotted out all else—making her tremble with need—and she clung to him, uttering a small gasp as his hands slid under the velour top, eagerly seeking her breasts, a deep groan of appreciation escaping him when he realised she wasn't wearing a bra. Automatically, she strained towards him, her head dropping back in full capitulation, so that his lips burned across her cheek to trail a line of searing kisses down to the small hollow of her throat.

'Does any other man make you feel like this?' His fingers were in the pale cascade of her hair, massaging, caressing it, as if he couldn't get enough of its silken texture, but she couldn't answer his ragged question, only with a deep, sensual shudder as he bent to sample the sweet ripeness of her breast.

She could feel his hard arousal through the towel as he pulled her hips against his—the velvet of his bare skin where her fingertips curled into his shoulders—and her stomach churned in an agony of wanting. No, no man had ever made her feel like this, she thought, reasoning vaguely, arching her back in response to the sweet torment of his tongue. Their physical chemistries together were explosive even without love between them—even though he could walk away from her afterwards and . . .

'No!' Suddenly she was tearing herself away from him, small choking sounds rising from her throat.

'What's wrong?' He looked hurt, the strong planes of his face clouded, bewildered.

'Gabrielle,' she gasped, flinging the name accusingly at him, keeping her eyes averted so that he wouldn't see the pain in them.

'Gaby?' He shook his head, his dark brows drawn together. 'What about her?' 'You're going to . . .' She broke off—couldn't bring herself to say it.

'Going to what?' he prompted with some impatience, looking perplexed.

'To . . . marry her . . . aren't you?' she quizzed, with a tentative glance at him. And was staggered when he literally threw back his head and laughed.

'What on earth gave you that idea?'

'Aren't you?' she persisted, confusion spinning with love and pain beneath a tidal wave of dangerous hope.

Frowning, Elliot shook his head. 'No . . . I'm not.'

'But Trudy's letter said . . .' Fleur paused, trying to restore some balance to her thoughts. 'Chris . . .' she went on. 'He told me that Gabrielle said . . . that she and you were engaged . . .'

He glanced away towards the fire. 'Oh . . . I see.' It was said with such cool acceptance that hope flooded out of her, leaving a deep chasm of emptiness inside.

So it's true, she thought. He'll have to admit it now.

His eyes, meeting the wounded darkness of hers were cool and unwavering. 'Gaby's been engaged to every man who's ever given her a second glance,' he stated, his mouth pulling down at one corner. 'That's a sad fact. Her mother died when Gaby was six and she's been insecure and looking for a stable relationship with someone ever since. I've known her a long time and that's the way I see it. The Colonel was always too involved with the army and his business ventures to take any real interest in her.' He shrugged. 'So she looked to the men in her life to fill the breach. And yes . . .' he announced, frankly, answering her unspoken question, 'I made love to her . . . but she knew the score. She knew I had no intention of settling

down with her. Then . . . kissing you; being with you . . .'
Under the dark triangle of hair she saw the hard chest
muscles flex and she blushed, remembering their
antagonised intimacy in the mews. 'I haven't touched
another woman since . . .'

She could hardly believe what he was saying. A deep
warmth was suffusing her body, making her glow inside.
'But you were horrible to me!' she exhaled, her dark eyes
wide—incredulous. 'And afterwards you treated me as
though I didn't exist. And when you did finally start
speaking to me again, you didn't say anything about . . .'

'I know,' he acknowledged, raking his fingers through
his hair. 'But I wanted to give you time.' There was a self-
deprecating curl to his lips. 'Accusing a woman of
something she didn't do and abducting her for it doesn't
make for a beautiful relationship. I was hoping that if I
let things lie for a while I could get you to feel some
respect for me again. That night . . . after Asquith's party
. . . I don't know how I stopped myself from taking you to
bed. God! I wanted to!' This with a deep, emotional
shudder. 'But not only had you had too much to drink
that night, I knew how you felt about Markham and I
didn't want you doing anything with me you'd have
regretted afterwards. I couldn't have stood that. I wanted
you to get him out of your system first. I thought you'd
begun to,' he went on, amazing her with how wrong his
interpretation of her feelings for David had been, 'but
that day you handed in your notice and said you were
going abroad . . . I thought you were going with him.
That's why I was so keen to see you go as soon as I could.
I was so . . . angry about it . . . jealous . . .'

Incredulously, Fleur stared at him, scarcely daring to
believe that she wasn't dreaming. So he hadn't intended
to humiliate her that night—his rejection of her had been
for entirely honourable reasons. But that he had wanted
her . . . afterwards . . . when he'd been so aloof . . .

'David was never anything more than a brother to me,' she admitted tremulously now, her tone subdued against the crackling logs, the distant wash of the ocean beyond the house. 'We grew up together ... here ...'

'But I thought he was ...'

'My lover?' she supplied, gazing fully at his strong, baffled features, and he nodded. She shook her head. 'That was something you decided for yourself. I just let you think it because you were so determined to. But I wouldn't have gone abroad with him anyway ...'

'And all the time I thought you were in love with him ... even though you did respond to me when I touched you. I thought that was a purely physical thing with you until tonight ... until I saw how hurt you were ...' Under the deep tan, Elliot's cheeks were tinged with colour, and his palms, lightly cupping her elbows, were drawing her towards him. Beneath the soft crimson, Fleur trembled, her hands against his bare chest, stalling him.

'How did you know that David was going abroad?' she puzzled, trying to think even though her fingers were itching to caress that mat of dark, wiry hair. As far as she could remember, she hadn't mentioned his going away to anyone at the office.

'The day I dismissed him I told him to get the hell out of the country if he wanted to avoid charges,' Elliot shocked her by saying. 'I didn't want him hurting you again.'

So that was it—she should have known! David would never have done anything quite as drastic as emigrating unless he'd been propelled by some will stronger than his own, she was certain of that. And that will had been Elliot's.

'I want you,' he said, his arms going around her, and she shuddered from the depth of emotion in his voice. 'I want you to be my woman ... mine and only mine ... I wanted to tell you that at that bus stop when you ran away from me . . .'

'But you were seeing Gaby that day!' she reminded him, perplexed, doubt pulling against the joy—the love—which was striving to be acknowledged. 'You admitted it yourself.'

'Purely for business purposes,' he enlightened her, pushing a soft, blonde tendril back from her flushed face. 'She had a message for me from her father . . . you know I'm taking over the Pylon Corporation which Asquith's own?' And seeing the astonishment in her face he said, amazed, 'Don't you ever watch television . . . read the papers? It's had headline coverage more than once.'

She couldn't tell him that she had stopped taking newspapers because it hurt too much to keep reading about him, and she seldom switched the television on. But she realised now what Trudy had meant when she'd referred to Elliot taking a big step—his takeover of a big corporation—and Pylon was huge! She hadn't been talking about marriage at all! What a fool she'd been . . .

'I've wanted you since the first day I saw you,' Elliot was saying, and she answered, with a tremulous little laugh,

'You mean the day you strode in and demanded a print-out without even bothering to say "please"?'

'Yes, then,' he breathed, trailing a finger along the soft outline of her cheek, making desire pulse through her as it moved to probe the trembling fullness of her lips. 'My lack of manners was inexcusable, but you'd knocked me so off balance I couldn't think straight. You were wearing a . . . a cream silk . . . shift . . . I think they call it, and all I could think about was how I could get you out of it.'

'You!' She admonished, laughingly, excitement threading through every nerve-ending in her body. He'd seemed so unapproachable—the type of man who would

never have given her a second glance—and all the time
he'd been nursing a latent desire of his own. With
admirable coolness, too. Rather shyly, she said, 'You
kept it very much to yourself.'

Elliot chuckled. 'The Chairman of the Board doesn't
ask one of his programmers to go to bed with him . . . not
on the very first meeting. And for the next couple of
months I decided I had to keep my mind on the business
rather than involve myself in a tempestuous affair with
you.'

She looked at him in mock disapproval. 'Is that what
you were planning?'

'Oh yes . . . very much so.' His breath was fanning the
smooth satin of her neck. 'In fact, that night I came into
your office and caught you innocently helping yourself to
my company's secrets, it was with the sole purpose of
asking you out to dinner. I knew you often worked late
and after attending to some business upstairs I decided to
take a chance on finding you still there . . . and alone.'
Her cheek against the darkening line of his jaw, she felt
rather than saw him grimace. 'I did . . . but it was one hell
of a shock when I discovered what you were doing and
thought you were trying to ruin everything my father
worked for. I could have beaten you crimson there and
then . . . and with less provocation than had you been
anyone else because I wanted you so much.'

His words seemed wrenched from him, and suddenly
he was crushing her to him, seeking her lips with a
desperation she hadn't felt in him before. His mouth
demanded, and she was yielding, passion building to
fever pitch inside her so that she was twisting her body to
make an easier passage for his hand to move under the
velour top, a throaty gasp escaping her as he found her
responsive breast and moulded it to his warm palm.
Pliable, softly panting, she collapsed against him, her
teeth nipping the hard flesh of his shoulder to relieve the

sweet torture of his massaging fingers, her nails softly clawing down over the velvety flesh of his back in a plea so strong it was almost audible.

'Not yet.' He was putting space between them— drawing her towards a chair—acknowledging her tangible disappointment by saying gently, 'There's plenty of time for this. I want to get to know you.' And she was on his lap, being cradled in his strong arms, a wonderful feeling of warmth and security enveloping her. 'I want to know everything about you. Your favourite literature. What you like to eat. Do you know I don't even know your middle name?'

'That's because I don't have one!' she said, laughingly. And shivered with delight as Elliot lifted her hair to place his lips against the nape of her neck.

'So that was why I couldn't find it on your file.'

'You mean you even *looked*!'

He'd shifted his position slightly so that her head was resting against his chest and she could feel the steady thud of his heartbeat—strong and regular.

'After our first meeting I was hungry for anything I could find about you ... craving information like a starving man craves food ... but office records weren't that informative.'

'And I thought you vetted everybody's files,' she confessed, shyly, remembering she'd suspected him of as much that night he'd first taken her to the mews. Elliot laughed, but Fleur couldn't now. That fresh, clean scent of him and the warmth of his bare skin were doing strange things to her equilibrium. Between the subtle light of one lamp and the glow from the fire, his chest gleamed a hard bronze, and tentatively she traced a path through the tangle of dark hair with her forefinger, fighting back the intense desire to touch it with her tongue.

'Did you mean what you said ... about Gabrielle?' she

asked, wanting reassurance.

And he murmured, 'Every word.'

'You hung her painting up . . .' She tilted her face to his, a soft pout to her lips. 'Even though you didn't like it.'

He grinned down at her, mouth twisting at her obvious jealousy. 'She hung it there,' he corrected, 'when she was helping me decorate the place. What did you imagine . . . that I made a hypocrite of myself just so I could get her into bed?'

Sheepishly, Fleur nodded. Well she had, hadn't she?

'You've got a very low opinion of me,' he growled softly, fingers catching in the silken cloud of loose hair. 'We were already casual lovers. I didn't have to do a devious thing like that to get my sex. I told her the damn thing was horrendous when she took it out of its wrapping, but she went ahead and hung it there anyway. And would you believe I didn't take it down because I didn't want to seem ungrateful . . . hurt her feelings?'

Fleur looked at him with teasing scepticism, shaking her head. And gasped as his fingers tightened with a gentle firmness in her hair.

'You've got a lot to learn,' he promised, the sensual threat in his voice exciting her. He eased her round to face him more, his dark features crossed by the shadows in the room, his eyes reflecting amber from the fire. 'I've been looking for you for weeks,' he surprised her by saying then, 'and I've been in a hell of a mood because I couldn't find you . . . I think I've upset just about everybody in the office. I called round to your flat a couple of days after I'd seen you in The Duke . . . it took me that forty-eight hours to come to terms with the fact that you might slam the door in my face . . . but your landlady said you'd moved out that morning and hadn't left any forwarding address. She seemed to think you were moving in with Caldridge.' His mouth tightened, and Fleur smiled to herself, guessing that the landlady had seen her stepping into Chris's car after he'd offered to drive her to the station. 'I even asked Trudy if she knew where you were but she said she didn't have a clue . . . although she came to me just half an hour before you rang and told me she'd got your address. You don't know the agony I've been through not knowing where you were . . .'

The agony he'd been through! She wanted to laugh—to speak—but she couldn't. Love, with desire, was making her weak and slightly heady, and she'd had enough of talking. She wanted to go to bed.

'Is it over between you and Caldridge?' It was a lightly put question, as though he had no doubt about the answer, and she murmured truthfully now,

'It hadn't even begun.'

'And tell me something else . . .' His voice had taken on a deep, sensual undertone as he tipped her back across his arm. 'Did you really toss my clothes over the cliff? Because if you did . . .' There was laughter in his eyes, but his words held a promise of some delightful punishment and Fleur touched her tongue to her top lip, a frisson shooting through her. Of course. He didn't like being out of control. And she was realising a sudden, reckless enjoyment in still having the better of him. She smiled provocatively up at him, her fingers finding their own enjoyment in an exploratory tour of his magnificent biceps as she taunted, daringly,

'Hadn't it occurred to you, my dear ex-boss, that if I keep you naked you'll be less inclined to run away?'

Her words were an echo from the past, and arousing in themselves, yet she wasn't fully expecting the strong reaction they incited. She was challenging his masculine dominance and he didn't like it, she realised too late, because his arms were tightening around her—crushing her to him, and his mouth was suddenly inflicting a

bruising pressure on hers that left her breathless—
vulnerable to its demands. She was out of her depth—
contending with a hard, male aggression she didn't know
how to control—trying to stay afloat, yet finding the hard
dominance of his mouth forcing her down into a deep,
warm pleasurable sea of sensation where pain was
ecstasy—awareness, a burning, throbbing need that
swelled in her loins and sent a violent explosion of want
through her entire body.

And suddenly he was sweeping her up out of the chair
with such violent purpose that in spite of her arousal she
trembled.

'I-I thought you wanted to talk,' she stammered,
stupidly.

'It can wait.' His breathing was heavy as he moved
instinctively and with determined strides to the room
with the double bed. 'I'll get to know you tomorrow.'

Sunlight streamed in from a hard, vivid sky. She could
hear the lazy wash of the ocean from what seemed a long
way off, and there was a mistiness to the window panes
which hinted at a cold, frosty day.

Drowsily, Fleur stirred between the warm sheets,
stretching her naked body with a sensual languor, a few
sensitive spots on the soft flesh bringing home the reality
of last night.

He had been tender in bed. But a brief adolescent
affair and celibacy since hadn't prepared her for the
storm of passion she'd met in his arms, or given her any
inkling as to the extent of her own, inhibited sexuality.
Experienced and unerringly patient, he had schooled her
through a long, luxurious night, laughing softly at her
own inexperience when she had tried to please him with
trembling, tentative fingers, gradually drawing her from
shyness to uninhibited actions which made her blush
now as she remembered them. But there had been only

one person in command last night. With a sensual shudder she recalled how he had brought her to the brink of ecstasy again and again, withholding it until she was sobbing and pleading with him for release. And when he had granted it, rocked out of control by his own urgent need, it was then she had cried out her love for him, taking him into her with a totally open heart so that he had been left in no doubt as to exactly how she felt about him. But where was he now?

Staring at the small depression in the pillow next to hers, a thin thread of anxiety began to tug at her. Last night she had committed herself to him completely, while Elliot hadn't mentioned one word of love. Not one whisper of any plans for the future. He'd said only that he wanted her to be his woman, although, contrarily, he'd said earlier that he hadn't wanted an affair. Well, he must have changed his mind, she thought, suddenly hurting unbelievably inside, because that was before he'd known she didn't feel anything for David . . .

'Good morning.'

Her gaze swivelled towards the doorway through which Elliot was striding, a cup and saucer in his hand. But it was his appearance which made Fleur sit up. A beige, chunky sweater was teamed with dark trousers and casual shoes, and his hair was freshly groomed. It was obvious he had shaved, too.

'You found your suit?' she breathed, clutching the bedclothes to her, suddenly shy. How else could he have got that change of clothes he'd obviously brought with him without first finding his car keys? And they were in the pocket of the trousers he'd been wearing last night. 'You got up early and went looking for it!'

'And rob you of your little triumph?' He laughed, placing the cup down on the bedside table before stooping to brush her lips with his and despite the brevity of the kiss, fresh desire stirred in her loins. 'Anyway . . . I thought you'd dumped it in the ocean.' He pulled an amused face and she knew her little game was up.

'I was going to,' she stated, emphatically, wanting him to know that that had been her full intention, 'but in the end I couldn't.' She lifted a smooth, bare shoulder, hoping she didn't look as sheepish as she felt admitting to having had second thoughts. 'I stuck it in the shed.' Her brown eyes ran questioningly over him. 'So how did you get those?',

He smiled. 'If you've ever locked your keys in your car, you'd know how embarrassing, *and* inconvenient it can be. I did it once and vowed it would never happen to me again. I keep a spare under the Jag.'

'You . . .!' Self-satisfaction was written all over his face and she had to restrain the strongest urge to whack him. In spite of all her plans to outwit him, *he'd* come out on top—literally!

'If I come closer will you promise not to attack me?' he grinned, clearly reading what was in her mind.

'You're devious,' she spat, and felt a wave of heat wash over her as Elliot sat down, the bed depressing under his weight.

'Not half as devious as you are!' he reminded her, his grey eyes holding laughter. She thought how handsome he was, his dark features strong—almost aristocratic—his perfect teeth white against his tan. He smelt nice, too, and she had to look away from him, knowing the sudden pain of wanting more of him than she could ever hope to have. 'A man in my position can't afford to take chances,' he said, half-jokingly, twisting a strand of blonde hair around his forefinger. 'I like to be prepared for any emergency.'

'Like having a change of clothes . . . and a bathrobe in the car?' she enquired, pointedly. 'Just in case your others get mislaid?'

'No . . . not only for that reason,' he said gently. 'When

Trudy told me where you were, I made up my mind to come down here last night even before you rang. When you did, I still wasn't sure whether I'd be able to make you want me like I wanted you, so I decided to stay down here last night anyway ... book into a hotel and come back and see you again today if I couldn't get you to accept me then.' He smiled. 'But you did.' He stroked the smooth satin of her neck with the back of his hand and a cool tremor ran through her.

Yes, she had accepted him. He'd got what he wanted. But what did she have now? Nothing, she thought, seeing him glancing at his watch.

'Unfortunately, business dictates that I get back by lunchtime,' he was explaining, and she guessed that he had read a little of the misery in her eyes. 'I've got a meeting with Colonel Asquith to discuss this wretched takeover ... so I'll have to be on the road soon.' He reached for the cup and saucer, and handed them to her. 'Drink your tea,' he said, rather dispassionately. 'It's getting cold.'

Silently, she obeyed. Was this what it was going to be like having an affair with him? she wondered, desolately. Having stolen nights of rapture torn cruelly away from her by businessmen and their beautiful daughters? Because Gaby would be there today, she was certain of that. And there would always be other Gabys—mature, sophisticated women who would offer him sex without emotional involvement as she would never be able to do. Could she stand such an insecure relationship, loving him so much and wondering all the time if this would be the day when he didn't come back ...

'If you aren't going to finish it,' his deep tones drawled through her unhappy thoughts, 'then you'd better start thinking about getting up. We should be leaving here by eight.'

'We?' Fleur echoed, her heart seeming to stand still.

'Well you are going to marry me, aren't you?' he asked, smiling down at her open-mouthed amazement. 'You can't rob me of my clothes and my honour without making an honest man of me.'

'Oh, Elliot . . .' She couldn't speak, too choked by the tears which were making her eyes sparkle like dark pools in sunlight. 'I thought you wouldn't . . . that you didn't . . .'

'Love you?' he provided, his thumbs brushing away the two silver beads which were trembling beneath her lower lids. Gently he lifted her small chin with his finger, tilting her head so that she was looking up into the darkened grey depths of his eyes. 'Did I forget to tell you that?'

She sniffed and nodded, giving him a tremulous smile, and he said, almost impatiently, shaking his head as though he couldn't believe her naïvety, 'Why on earth do you think I've been trying so hard to find you? I love you Fleur.' His voice was husky with emotion. 'I love your warmth, your beauty, your spirit. Even your damned loyalty to David. I think I even loved you all the time I was holding you at the mews . . . even though at the time I could quite easily have wrung your precious little neck! But I'm glad now I didn't.' He laughed, gathering her to him. 'Seriously, darling, I said I'm not a man to take chances and we took one last night.' And more softly, 'Two if I remember correctly.' Colour stole into her cheeks from the reminder of their reckless lovemaking, and where the bedclothes had fallen away she could feel the urgent response of her breasts against Elliot's rough sweater. 'I think we'd better get married before we start to reap the consequences.'

'Would you like that?' she asked, tentatively, realising that she had no idea about his views on children, or marriage for that matter.

'I'm thirty-six,' he said. 'I'd like to start a family as

soon as I can . . . that's if you don't mind. Of course, if
you'd rather pursue a career . . .'

'No I . . .' She felt dazed. Everything was happening so
fast. But she was certain about one thing, and whispered,
guilelessly, 'I'd like your child more than anything else in
the world.'

Crushed in his arms, she was his prisoner again—
knew she always would be—but a prisoner of love held
by bonds far stronger than any she could touch or feel or
see. And when he pushed her back against the pillows,
tugging off his sweater to feel her yielding nakedness
against his, she knew only total surrender to her captor as
he murmured, excitingly, glancing at his watch, 'I think
we'd better make that twenty-past.'

Harlequin Romance

Coming Next Month

Available in April wherever paperback books are sold, or through Harlequin Reader Service.

In the U.S.
P.O. Box 1397
Buffalo, N.Y.
14240-1397

In Canada
P.O. Box 603
Fort Erie, Ontario
L2A 5X3

ATTRACTIVE, SPACE SAVING BOOK RACK

Display your most prized novels on this handsome and sturdy book rack. The hand-rubbed walnut finish will blend into your library decor with quiet elegance, providing a practical organizer for your favorite hard-or soft-covered books.

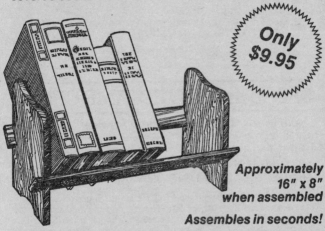

Only $9.95

**Approximately
16" x 8"
when assembled**

Assembles in seconds!

To order, rush your name, address and zip code, along with a check or money order for $10.70* ($9.95 plus 75¢ postage and handling) payable to *Harlequin Reader Service*:

> Harlequin Reader Service
> Book Rack Offer
> 901 Fuhrmann Blvd.
> P.O. Box 1325
> Buffalo, NY 14269-1325

Offer not available in Canada.

BKR-1R

*New York residents add appropriate sales tax.

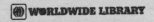